D1483761

✦ Son-of-Thunder

Son-of-Thunder

Stig Holmås

Translated by Anne Born

Illustrations by John Hurford

Harbinger House
TUCSON

HARBINGER HOUSE, INC.
Tucson, Arizona

© 1993 Harbinger House
All rights reserved
Manufactured in the United States of America
∞ This book is printed on acid-free, archival-quality paper
Edited and designed by Harrison Shaffer

10 9 8 7 6 5 4 3 2 1

First published in 1985 under the title
Tordensønnen by Gyldendal Norsk Forlag, Oslo
© Gyldendal Norsk Forlag

This edition is published by special arrangement
with Spindlewood, Barnstaple Devon, Great Britain.

Library of Congress Cataloging-in-Publication Data
Holmås, Stig, 1946–
    [Tordensonnen. English]
    Son-of-Thunder / Stig Holmås ; translated by Anne Born ;
illustrations by John Hurford.
        p. cm.
    Summary: During the time of Cochise and Geronimo, an adopted
Apache boy joins in the desperate struggle of his people to hold
their hunting grounds in southern Arizona against alien invaders.
    ISBN 0-943173-88-4 (HC) :   —ISBN 0-943173-87-6 (PB) :
    1. Apache Indians—Juvenile fiction. [1. Apache Indians—
Fiction. 2. Indians of North America—Southwest, New—Fiction.]
I. Hurford, John, ill.   II. Title.
PZ7.H7328So 1993
[Fic]—dc20   93-4211

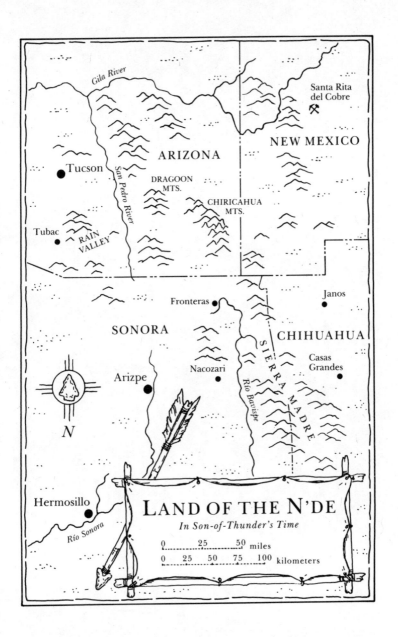

Gila River

Santa Rita
del Cobre

NEW MEXICO

ARIZONA

Tucson

DRAGOON
MTS.

San Pedro River

CHIRICAHUA
MTS.

Tubac

RAIN
VALLEY

Janos

Fronteras

SONORA

CHIHUAHUA

Nacozari

Casas
Grandes

Arizpe

SIERRA MADRE

Río Bavispe

N

Hermosillo

LAND OF THE N'DE

In Son-of-Thunder's Time

Río Sonora

0   25   50 miles

0   25   50   75   100 kilometers

◆ *Part I: The Rain Valley*

✦ Son-of-Thunder

On the night a thunderstorm raged above the land of the N'de Indians, Little Eagle gave birth to her first child. Her husband, Swift Deer, stood in the shelter of an overhanging cliff gazing at their home, a wickiup built of twigs. At his side was his father-in-law, old Elk Heart. The rain slashed at the earth; violent gusts of wind tore at bushes and trees. Blue lightning ripped into the dark and the thunderclaps echoed and rolled around the mountains. Elk Heart looked anxiously up into the darkness and prayed in a low voice:

> *"Hear my voice, Grandfather Lightning.*
> *Be kind to us poor humans*
> *as you pass by.*
> *Do not frighten the newborn one*
> *and do not harm him.*
> *Let all be well when you have gone."*

Between the peals of thunder Swift Deer could hear the faint crying of the newborn child in the wickiup and his heart beat fiercely. He and Little Eagle had been married many years, but this was their first child. Swift Deer was glad his father-in-law was praying. Elk Heart was a wise man and everyone knew he was a friend of the gods.

Swift Deer was tall, sinewy, and strong. He wore leather clothes and ankle-length moccasins. His long black hair was held back from his face by a headband of light-colored deerskin.

Suddenly the twig door that covered the low entrance to the wickiup was pushed open and Good Care, the old midwife, crawled out into the darkness. She rose and walked out into the storm. Her face was lit up by the blue lightning flashes and Swift Deer could see she was smiling. She stopped in front of the two men. Her wet hair was long and gray. She was slight, and her face was full of wrinkles and furrows. She met Swift Deer's questioning gaze.

"Be joyful, Swift Deer," she said ceremoniously. "This night Little Eagle has borne you a son. He is a fine big boy. We sang and prayed that the Thunder People should not harm him but give him a good body and a long life. Little Eagle is tired now, but all is well with mother and child."

Then Swift Deer threw his arms around the old woman and thanked her. He had never felt so happy in his life.

"It is not for me to decide," said Good Care when he let her go, "but if he was my boy I would honor the powers that are abroad tonight and call him Son-of-Thunder."

Swift Deer looked inquiringly at his father-in-law and Elk Heart nodded.

"Son-of-Thunder is a good name," he said.

"Son-of-Thunder is a good name," repeated Swift Deer. "That's what he will be called."

Good Care turned back to the hut while Swift Deer went to stay the night with his father-in-law. The storm passed away to the north and the next day dawned still and warm. The sun shone and steam rose from the wet earth. Good Care stayed with Little Eagle and Son-of-Thunder in the twig wickiup, but when Swift Deer came to visit them she went out and left the three of them alone. The newborn boy lay with closed eyes and nursed at his mother's heavy breast. Swift Deer had never seen anything more beautiful. He felt how the sight of the helpless little creature filled him with tenderness and goodness.

Little Eagle and Son-of-Thunder lay safe and warm under a big fur. Swift Deer squatted down beside them.

"He takes after you," said Little Eagle.

Swift Deer stroked her forehead gently.

"He takes after you too," he said.

Little Eagle looked at her husband and smiled. He smiled back. No two people could love each other more than they did.

Lightning can smash stones and split trees. And that afternoon Swift Deer made his way up into the forest-clad mountains west of the valley where they lived. His bow was slung over his shoulder and his arrows were in a quiver on his back. The quiver was made of prairie wolf skin. A sheath knife hung from a belt around his waist. Tall pine trees stretched their twisted boughs toward the sky, and after a few hours he found what he was searching for, the trunk of an old pine tree that had been shattered by lightning from crown to root. Swift Deer took out his knife and cut off a small piece of the white hardwood. When he got home he would bore a hole in it and thread a leather thong through it. Then he would hang it on Son-of-Thunder's cradle, the one Elk Heart had promised to make, for amulets of a pine tree struck by lightning bring luck to newborn N'de.

Swift Deer wrapped the piece of wood in a cloth of soft deerskin and packed it carefully in his quiver. Then he climbed to the top of a peak with a view in all directions. Below to the east of him he saw parts of the fertile Rain Valley where he and some of the other N'de had their homes. They stood along a stream among peaceful willow trees; about forty people lived in the valley. Before Swift Deer set off, all of them, old and young, had come to congratulate him on the birth of his son.

Swift Deer could see more pine-clad mountains on the other side of the Rain Valley. Away to the east and west the dry prairies stretched out as far as the eye could see. To the north lay the yellow-brown desert, a low belt of green cactus-covered ridges and distant blue mountain ranges with sharp peaks. To the south too he could see mountains. And he knew that beyond all this lay other deserts, other prairies, forests, mountains, valleys, streams, rivers, and waters. Everywhere were animals and plants that could be eaten or used in various ways.

Once upon a time only Indians had lived in this huge country. Swift Deer and his family belonged to one of the many small groups of N'de. N'de means "the people," but others called them Apache, which means "enemy." They lived by hunting and gathering, or on what they took as booty on raids or in warfare.

The N'de were skilled warriors. They often defeated a superior enemy by their cunning. They knew every inch of their land, the hidden paths and hiding places.

They lured their enemy into traps, always attacked when he was off guard, and withdrew at lightning speed.

The Mexicans had long ago come north to these lands and settled here. They were more numerous than the N'de and they had fire-weapons which could kill from a great distance. Fire-weapon was the Indian name for gun. The Mexicans plundered and killed and tried to take over the country, but the N'de fought back. The fighting still went on, but the Mexicans had had to give up many of their settlements. They left behind them deserted farms, villages, and towns. Only in a few places did they hang on. Soldiers kept watch behind cannons by day and night.

"When Son-of-Thunder is old enough I will tell him about all our victories over the Mexicans," thought Swift Deer. "I will bring him up to this mountaintop and show him how beautiful our land is."

Swift Deer took off his bow and arrows and sat down. He thought about Son-of-Thunder and the world he was born into.

Now other strange peoples too were beginning to appear in the N'de lands. The N'de called these people "white eyes" and the Mexicans called them *Norteamericanos.* They came from north and east and had pale skin and hair on their faces. They were few in number and all were hunters. They were friendly and were received as guests. One of them was called Red Hair. He had taught himself N'de language and married a N'de woman. Red Hair had told them of a great lake far away to the east. On the other side of this lake were many countries with big towns. All the white eyes had come from over there. The lake was called the Atlantic Ocean, and Red Hair had been born in a place called England. The N'de liked Red Hair and mourned him when he died.

But the Mexicans were different. They never tried to learn the N'de language. They only wanted to take over N'de country. Elk Heart had heard that now the Mexicans were recruiting soldiers for a great army to fight against the N'de.

"Perhaps one day they will come here to the Rain Valley too," Elk Heart had said. "They have new fire-weapons and long knives they call swords, and they come riding big swift horses. They bring a cloth with them that is fastened to a pole. It is green, white, and red, and one of the soldiers blows on a horn of shining metal before they attack. The sound of the horn is a death song, and the Mexicans want our blood to redden the grass."

Swift Deer sat on the mountaintop and thought about what Elk Heart had said, but he also remembered something he had heard since. In the northeast the N'de chief Red Sleeves had chased Mexican soldiers southward into the desert toward Chihuahua. He had swept the little mining town of Santa Rita del Cobre clean of Mexicans, and N'de came from afar to fight with him. Perhaps it might be possible to drive the Mexicans out for good.

"Then Son-of-Thunder can grow up in a free country," thought Swift Deer. "I will teach him to find his way through the desert, in the forests, in the mountains and on the prairie. I will teach him the names of animals and plants, teach him to know the birds by their song. He will learn to follow a trail and read the signs of the heavens and earth. I will give him a bow, arrows, and a horse. He will be a rider, hunter, and warrior. I will teach him to respect the earth and all life. He will never kill more creatures than he needs."

Swift Deer sat there and smiled.

"Son-of-Thunder and I will be the best friends in the world," he thought.

The sun sank low in the west and a gentle evening breeze played with his hair. He watched an eagle sail off on wide wings, heard a coyote howl. In the wickiup down in the Rain Valley Son-of-Thunder lay safe and warm under the big fur.

"I have not seen his eyes yet," thought Swift Deer. "They must be as big and beautiful as his mother's. I will teach him to use those eyes well."

Swift Deer pictured how Son-of-Thunder would grow into a strong young man, how they would ride out one day to a fertile valley full of game. *Suddenly Son-of-Thunder signaled for them to stop. They jumped down from their horses and Son-of-Thunder squatted down and pointed at something in the tall grass. It was a little piece of dung. Swift Deer had not noticed it, but his son had the eye of a hawk. The dropping was almost globe-shaped with a little point. It was black and covered with shiny mucus. Son-of-Thunder touched it carefully with his fingers and looked at his father.*

"It is from a deer, and it is warm," he said. "We'll have deer meat tonight, Father."

"You have keen eyes," said Swift Deer proudly.

There he sat on the mountaintop dreaming and making plans.

The two of them rode on through the valley, found the deer, and Son-of-Thunder dropped it with an arrow he had made of mesquite. Swift Deer smiled with pleasure and nodded to his son.

"You have keen eyes," he said, "but you're an even better shot."

"Thank you," said Son-of-Thunder, "but my hearing is better still. I think we should be getting home. Can you hear the thunder?"

Swift Deer listened. Yes, now he heard it. The rumbling of a distant thunderstorm. Or was it really thunder? Wasn't it the sound of . . .

And abruptly Swift Deer was shaken out of his dream and the lush valley. He was back on the mountaintop and it was no thunder he heard but the faint drumming of heavy galloping animals. Could it be cattle? No, none of the N'de had ridden out to raid.

Swift Deer stood up, listened, and looked around. Then he caught sight of them, far down there to the north on the way to the valley and his home, hundreds of moving horses. They were not wild; they were not running in a herd. They came galloping in a long row, two by two, side by side, and men were riding them. At first he could not see the riders clearly—the distance was too great and the horses' hooves churned up the dust around them. But then he caught sight of the green, white, and red cloth on the long pole and saw the sunlight flash on the long knives. Swift Deer remembered what Elk Heart had said.

"Perhaps one day they will come to our valley too. They have new fire-weapons and long knives they call swords, and they come riding on big swift horses. They bring a cloth with them fastened to a pole. It is green, white, and red, and one of the soldiers blows a horn of shining metal before they attack. The sound of the horn is a death song, and the Mexicans want our blood to redden the grass."

Suddenly Swift Deer was filled with fear, deathly fear.

"Little Eagle and Son-of-Thunder are in danger!" the thought shot through his head. "Elk Heart and all my neighbors! I must warn them! The Mexicans are attacking!"

He bent quickly, seized bow and arrows, and ran. Down from the mountaintop, down among the stones and into the pine forest. Down, down. Faster, faster. He ran and ran. His heart was thumping; the blood coursed through his veins. Faster, faster. The birds flew up from the trees around him; a hare vanished among the tree trunks. And while Swift Deer ran, he prayed. He prayed to all the powers and gods the N'de knew, to the Mountain People, the Thunder People, and the mightiest of them all, Usen, he who had created all the N'de.

"Hear my prayer, great Usen. Help me to warn all those I love. Give me eagle's wings. I must run faster, faster. Let me be worthy of my name. Hear my prayer, great Usen. Let me help Son-of-Thunder and Little Eagle! Son-of-Thunder! Let me get there in time!"

Then he heard the death song from the soldiers' shining horn, an evil and fearful song. He reached the edge of the trees and rushed at top speed out on to the flat space of the valley bottom. There were the wickiups under the willow trees. He saw terrified N'de trying to flee in all directions. He saw Little Eagle creep from their wickiup with Son-of-Thunder in her arms, held close to her.

And he saw the Mexican soldiers shooting and shooting with their fire-weapons, slashing and slashing with their long knives. The snorting horses and mules kicked children and adults to the ground.

"Stop!" shouted Swift Deer in despair. "Stop! Don't hurt Son-of-Thunder! Don't hurt my wife!"

But the soldiers did not hear his cries; those storming men in blue uniforms and white cotton garb were deaf to them. They rode with long knives aloft, with fire-weapons that thundered and thundered among the wickiups in the hidden valley. And one of them, a man with a dark crooked scar on one cheek, aimed at Little Eagle as she ran bent low toward the bushes above the sloping river bank. He took aim and fired, and Swift Deer knew Little Eagle was dead when her body reached the slope. Son-of-Thunder rolled helplessly over the grass and lay there among the stamping hooves. Swift Deer raced across the valley, bent down, picked up his new-born son, and ran toward the brush. Shots were exploding everywhere, bullets like death-dealing swarms of mosquitoes filled the air, and suddenly Swift Deer felt a violent pain in his back. He knew he was hit and felt the blood stream down his back and his shirt stick to his body. But he went on running with clenched teeth while the pain almost drove him out of his senses. He ran and ran, into the scrub, down the slope, into the river, through the water, using every ounce of strength, into another thicket on the other side, up through the big stones into the talus, all the time with Son-of-Thunder in his arms . . .

✦ *Swift Deer and Good Care*

It was slowly growing light again.

First he recognized the smell of smoke, then he could see. A bit of the sky, some of the big stones on the slope, and Good Care's old face.

He lay in shadow but there was light and warmth around him. It must be midday. He remembered running toward the river, the bullet hitting him in the back. It had been early evening then. He had waded across to the other side with Son-of-Thunder in his arms and reached the stones. Then everything had gone black.

Good Care bent down and spoke to him.

"Can you hear me, Swift Deer?"

He opened his mouth to reply but could not make a sound. His tongue was swollen, his palate dry, his throat sore. Good Care gave him water from a pottery beaker. He swallowed a little. He could whisper.

"Yes, I can hear you. How is my son?"

"Asleep," answered Good Care. "I have given him water boiled with herbs."

"Is he hurt?"

"No, he is unhurt, and well. He is sleeping peacefully now."

"But Little Eagle is dead?"

"Yes."

Swift Deer wept silently. The tears ran down his face on to the deerskin he lay on. Little Eagle was dead, and Wild Cat, Good Care's only son, had fallen too. He knew that without asking her, for Good Care had cut her hair off short, as was the custom when a close relative died.

"And the others?" whispered Swift Deer.

Good Care made no reply.

"Are they dead?"

She still did not answer.

"The others," repeated Swift Deer, "are they dead?"

Now there were tears in Good Care's eyes too.

"Yes," she said.

"All of them?" Swift Deer couldn't believe it.

"Yes."

Swift Deer closed his eyes and breathed painfully. All of them. Dead, all of them. Little Eagle, Wild Cat, Elk Heart, all his friends and neighbors, Little Eagle's family. Where had the gods been? Why did not Usen let me get there in time? Why am I lying here with a lifeless body? Swift Deer opened his eyes again. An icy fear seized him.

"Am I going to die too?" he whispered.

No reply.

"Answer me, Good Care. Am I going to die too?" he repeated.

Then, "Yes, Swift Deer," she said. "You too are going to die. Your back is broken, your blood has run out into the sand. I have done what I could, but the blue shadow is spreading over your body."

Then Swift Deer remembered what he had dreamed and thought about on the mountaintop. So he would not after all be able to teach Son-of-Thunder to find his way through the desert, across the prairie, and in the mountains. And he would not be able to teach his son the names of animals and plants, teach him to know the birds by their songs. He would never give him a bow, arrows, and a horse. Never would they ride out to hunt together in a valley thick with game.

"But he will be a rider, hunter, and warrior all the same," said Swift Deer, and suddenly his voice was louder and clearer, almost as before.

"What do you mean, Swift Deer?" asked Good Care.

The dying brave met her eyes.

"Are we safe here? Have the soldiers gone?"

"Yes, they set fire to everything and rode off southward right away yesterday evening."

Swift Deer took thought. Then he said, "Will you do what I ask you, will you take Son-of-Thunder with you to a good, safe place?"

Now his voice was weaker again, and Good Care gave him some more water.

"You and your wife were always kind to me, and my son had nothing but good to say of you, Swift Deer," she said. "Besides, it was I who prayed to the gods and gave my help when Son-of-Thunder was born the night before last. And was it not I who suggested his name as well? What do you want me to do?"

Swift Deer smiled faintly.

"You are a fine woman, Good Care."

He closed his eyes again, and now he saw himself as a small boy among the trees in a valley far to the north. He saw wickiups and people around little fires, he saw his parents and his eldest brother, strong tall Nachi.*

---

*Not to be confused with Naiche, Cochise's son.

And he remembered how Nachi had always looked after him and prepared him for the four raids all N'de boys must go out on before they can become warriors. Swift Deer thought of how he had met Little Eagle, the most beautiful woman he had ever seen. They had married and Swift Deer had moved south to her family in the Rain Valley, as was the custom.

He opened his eyes again.

"I want you to take Son-of-Thunder and travel north to the Chiricahua Mountains. My brother Nachi is there; he is chief of all the Chokonen.† Tell him my last great wish was that Nachi should bring up Son-of-Thunder as his own child."

"Of course I know your brother," said Good Care, "but it is a long way to the Chiricahua Mountains, and I am old, Swift Deer. The Mexican soldiers took away all our horses, so I will have to make my way on foot."

"Yes, it is true your body is old, but your will is young and strong. I know you can do it if you try," said Swift Deer.

They kept silence again for a while. Swift Deer could feel the last of his strength ebbing away.

"In my quiver there is a piece of pine tree struck by lightning. Tell Nachi, and Son-of-Thunder when he is old enough, that was why I was up in the mountains the day the Mexican soldiers came."

"That I promise to do," said Good Care.

"I want you to make a hole in the piece of wood. I want you to thread a leather thong through it and hang it on Son-of-Thunder's cradle. When he gets bigger he must wear it around his neck. Say I sat up on the moun-

---

†The Chokonen were also known as the Central Chiricahua Band.

taintop and dreamed of how we would one day go hunting together. I would show him how beautiful our lands are. It was then I heard the Mexican soldiers coming. Say that I ran and ran to warn you all, that I prayed to the gods and thought of him and his mother, but I was still too late getting there."

Swift Deer's voice grew weaker and weaker as he spoke and Good Care had to put her ear close to his mouth to catch the words.

"Do not worry. I promise to do everything you have said."

"Good," said Swift Deer. "Now, will you do me one favor while I still live? I want to see Son-of-Thunder. Go get him."

So Good Care rose, fetched the newborn boy and held him out before his dying father. Swift Deer opened his eyes for the very last time, and Son-of-Thunder too had opened his. They were big and beautiful and just like Little Eagle's.

✦ Northward

That evening Good Care reached the end of the Rain Valley. To her north lay the desert. She decided to camp under a big oak tree. She had wrapped up Son-of-Thunder in a warm fur, and now she carefully put him down on the grass. The sun painted the sky deep red and somewhere out in the wide evening landscape the coyotes began to howl.

The Mexican soldiers had set fire to all the wickiups before they left. But the flames had not devoured everything and Good Care had gone around searching among the charred remains of the N'de homes. She had found some skins, a clay cooking pot, some bags of herbs, and two water bags. One of these she filled from the river; the other she left empty. She took Swift Deer's bow and arrows with her too.

She found some round stones in the grass and made a fireplace. Then she gathered dry twigs and set fire to them with two little flints she always had with her. She poured water into the pot, added some herbs and placed the pot on the fire. While she waited for it to boil she thought over what had happened. She had buried Wild Cat, Little Eagle, and Swift Deer among the stones on the slope. The others she left lying where the Mexicans had killed them. Then she had taken Son-of-Thunder in her arms and set off.

When the water and herbs had boiled for a while she took the pot off the fire and set it on the grass to cool. Then she poured it into the empty water bag. Next she picked up Son-of-Thunder and held him on her lap. She bit a tiny hole in the bag for the baby to suck from. He should really be having milk from a woman's breast, but he would have to wait a while for that.

When he had had enough she held him up and stroked his back till he burped. Then she put him on her lap again and sang softly:

> *"Hush, my lonesome little child.*
> *Hush, my lonesome little child."*

She sat on her haunches and rocked her body back and forth in time to the song. She was dressed in buckskin, a poncho, and a knee-length tunic. On her feet she wore high moccasins. She had a sheath knife stuck into one of them. Around her neck on leather thongs hung necklaces and amulets of mother-of-pearl, stones, bones, and wood.

Son-of-Thunder soon fell asleep and Good Care gently put him down again on the ground. Then she fetched more wood for the fire. Both mountain lions and rattlesnakes are afraid of fire, so she lay down just beside the fire with Son-of-Thunder close to her. Soon the old woman fell asleep too.

She was up before the sun. When the first rosy beams of day lit up the eastern sky she set off again. Son-of-Thunder had had more to drink and she held him in her arms while she ran. For Good Care did not walk, she ran, as the N'de always did when they were not on horseback. She did not run fast, but steadily, bent forward slightly at an almost tripping pace. As if she somehow fell forward with each step. On her back she carried the water bags, the quiver, and her few small belongings wrapped up in two skins. The bow hung over one shoulder, and Son-of-Thunder slept in her arms.

When the sun peered over the horizon she was already far north out in the desert. The sun rose; the air and the sand grew warm. She stopped once, took the water bag from her back and gave Son-of-Thunder a drink. She did not drink a drop herself. Then she ran on. Far ahead in the heat haze she saw the sharp contours of a yellow mesa, a table-shaped mountain in the midst of the sandy expanse. There she could rest. But the mountain was several hours off, and the sun rose higher and higher. The sweat poured off her body; she felt the poncho sticking to her back. Son-of-Thunder began to cry, but he was still sheltered in the shadow of the old woman's body. For the sun climbed in the south and Good Care ran northward. She stopped once more, gave him more water, wetted his hot little body. This time she drank a little herself as well.

She reached the mesa at midday. It was more than a hundred meters high with steep sides. She went on past it and came into the shadow of the north face, in among the hardy trees of a little thicket. A desert mouse rushed for safety under a stone; insects played over a small water hole. Otherwise the landscape seemed lifeless, though Good Care knew that in fact it was not. For scorpions and other crawling creatures lived out here in the desert, and there were hawks, foxes, and prairie wolves. During the day they hid away from the burning sun, but at night they came out of their shadows and dens to hunt and eat. That was why Good Care had decided to cross the desert in daylight. In the dark it would be impossible to see a poisonous rattlesnake or a mountain lion on the prowl. Besides this, all the N'de feared the nighttime, for if anyone was killed at night he was condemned to an eternity of endless wandering.

But now at midday, with the sun at the height of its power, it was too hot to go on. She herself could probably stand the cruel heat, but not Son-of-Thunder. So she set herself to wait patiently until late afternoon before going on northward. And when the dusk came creeping she reached the other side of the land of sand and settled down to rest among the green cactus of a hillside.

"This is the fourth day of your life, little one," said Good Care the next morning. "This is Cradle Day, but you don't know that. Today someone should have made a cradle for you, do you know that? No, you don't know that either, do you? But that is the custom with your people. The fourth day, that is Cradle Day. But you'll have to wait for your cradle till we get you to your uncle."

The land rose now, like a long billowing carpet of tinder-dry brown grass and small scattered bushes, rose up and up until it became a blue chain of mountains, the same mountains Swift Deer had seen when he sat dreaming that last day of his life.

✦ A Gift from Usen

A little old woman ran and ran with a baby clutched to her breast, one woman in a huge landscape of gigantic mountains, but with no sound of running feet, for Good Care sprinted silent as a cat through canyons and valleys. But she ached all over; her arms were stiff and sore from carrying the little one. The water bags and skins dug into her back; the sweat ran down.

The sun blazed. Again it was noon; again she found a resting place in the shade. Son-of-Thunder's body burned with fever, but he would not drink. She wetted his skin carefully and whispered to him anxiously.

"Hold on, little man. Only one more day, perhaps two, then we'll be there."

Perhaps two? She took fright at her own words. The furrow between her eyes deepened. No, two days was too long. She *had* to find the Chokonen by tomorrow. Son-of-Thunder needed a nurse. Milk from a woman's breast would give him strength. He was weak now and his fever was worse.

Good Care knew this country. By the evening she would be out of the mountains, would reach the plain. And north of that were the two big mountain ranges, the Dragoons and the Chiricahuas. But where were the Chokonen? Where were Nachi and his people? It was many years since Good Care had been in these parts. But all the same she knew every peak, every valley, all the streams and springs, every single hiding place. For what she had not seen herself, others had described. That was how it was with the N'de. They ran as no other people in this world had ever run and they knew their country. They roamed around in big and small groups, changed their hunting grounds, and found new places to live.

For a while they lived here, for a while there. This was Nachi and the Chokonen's habit too. Good Care knew that. They might be in the Dragoon Mountains at one time, at another in the Chiricahua Mountains. Now and then they would go even further afield, not just the warriors on raids or battles, but all of them, young and old, women and children. Good Care put Son-of-Thunder down on the grass.

"We'll try the Chiricahua Mountains," she muttered. "Your father thought we would find him there."

A little stream ran through the narrow valley where Good Care was resting. There were grass and flowers there, bushes and a few trees. She went down to the stream and drank. She filled the water bags.

Suddenly she stiffened. What was that? She had heard something. Wasn't it the sharp sound of a horse's hoof against a stone, the sound of a shod horse in movement? Like lightning she ran to Son-of-Thunder, swept him up in one arm, gathered her belongings in the other, and hid herself behind a rock.

Now she heard the horse snort. It came nearer. There was a bend in the valley northward, fifty or sixty steps away. The sound came from there. Good Care took thought. If the horse was shod it could not belong to a N'de, no, not to any Indian. For the Indians did not shoe their horses. So it was a Mexican, or perhaps a white eye. There weren't many white eyes. Good Care had met only a few. She could remember Red Hair.

The horse came nearer. Good Care sat perfectly still. Son-of-Thunder lay beside her. His eyes were closed.

"Great Usen," the old woman prayed silently, "don't let him wake up now. Don't let him cry. Let him sleep."

She heard the hooves on the grass. The horse snorted again; saddle leather creaked.

"Whoa, there," said a man's voice.

"He's going to the stream to drink," thought Good Care.

Soundlessly she took the bow from her shoulder, an arrow from the quiver. She laid the arrow carefully against the deer-sinew bowstring and tightened the bow. Then she crept out from behind the rock.

He was a Mexican. He was big and broad-shouldered and he was a soldier, dressed in the Mexican uniform. He had dismounted and was going toward the stream. Swiftly and silently Good Care stole up behind him. A wind had risen. A gentle breeze touched her face. Good. The horse would not smell her. She stopped a mere ten or fifteen steps from the Mexican's broad back. Hate rose in her; she tensed the bow a little more and then let the arrow fly. It lodged itself deep in the soldier and he was dead on the instant. Then she ran the last few steps and seized the horse's reins.

That night she rode across the plain toward the Chiricahua Mountains with Son-of-Thunder in front of her on the horse's back. The wind had strengthened to a

fresh breeze. Dark clouds hid the moon and stars, and
the horse's mane and her hair streamed in the darkness.
What had a soldier been doing alone out there in the
mountains to the south? The Mexicans seldom rode
alone in N'de country, and Mexican soldiers never. At
first she had thought he was a scout, one who rode
ahead of the main troop. So she had taken a different
route, higher up, found lookout places and tried to
catch sight of more soldiers. But the Mexican had been
alone, and Good Care thought that must have been
Usen's work.

"Usen wants you to live, Son-of-Thunder," she spoke
into the darkness. "He wants us to ride, to go faster.
That's why he sent the soldier. He wanted us to ride."

When the morning sun rose over the horizon they
rode in among strange yellow and reddish brown mountains, carved by divine hands to resemble giant sculp-
tures in the landscape. Nowhere were there so many
hiding places as here in the Chiricahua Mountains, nowhere so many traps for enemies of the N'de. Once
more she stopped by a stream, dismounted, and felt
Son-of-Thunder's forehead. He was still feverish. His little bird's heart beat with quick, feeble strokes.

Good Care laid him on the hillside and gathered
sticks for a big fire. The wind had dropped. She wetted
a deerskin in the stream. She was going to send up
smoke signals to tell them she was coming, but even
before she had lit the fire she knew they had discovered
her. Not that she had seen anything. Not that she had
heard anything. She just knew they were near, quite
close. She just felt it. For the N'de lived at one with
nature, were a part of it, and Good Care had instincts
that now only the animals have preserved.

All the same she lit the fire, covered it with the wet skin, and sent up big and little puffs of smoke. When she had finished she fetched the cooking pot and the water bags and got out the bag of dried herbs.

She was sitting on her haunches with Son-of-Thunder on her lap when they came. She still did not hear them, but she knew they were there. She rose and turned around with Son-of-Thunder in her arms.

There were three of them. They were all N'de, all warriors. One was very young, but taller and stronger than his companions. He wore a headband of red silk. The other two had leather headbands and long-sleeved leather tunics and loincloths. The young one wore only a loincloth. All carried bows and arrows, clubs and knives. But they did not wear war paint and were not holding their weapons at the ready. They just stood there. Silent. They stared at the old woman and the baby.

"I am Good Care," she said, "and this is Son-of-Thunder, Nachi's nephew."

Then the young brave gave her a friendly smile.

"And my cousin," he said. "For I am Cochise, son of Nachi."

✦ *Little Beaver*

Little Beaver sat by herself and wept. Down in the valley the other Chokonen were working outside their wickiups. Now and then they sent a sympathetic glance toward the sorrowing woman, but no one went up there to comfort her. They left her in peace. They thought that was best. Nachi, Little Beaver's husband, had stroked her hair kindly and told her to find some work to do.

"I grieve as well," he had said, "but there is nothing else for us to do but go on living as we have always done."

But Little Beaver found she could not work. Two years ago she had lost her first child, and a week ago they had buried the second. Both had been born weak and sickly and the second one, a beautiful little boy, had lived for barely a week.

"Why do you not allow my children to live, you gods?" whispered Little Beaver. "Give me a sign and tell me why."

She sat on a tree trunk up on the mountainside, an old oak that had fallen in the last thunderstorm. Down in the valley the women were busy with handcrafts or cooking. The braves made tools and weapons, and the children played among the wickiups.

"Why can't my children grow up to be healthy and lively like those?" thought Little Beaver. "What have I done wrong to be punished like this?"

Little Beaver was only twenty-four. Her husband had daughters who were older than she was. They were all children of Rain Woman, Nachi's eldest wife. The two women got on well together and Rain Woman had joined in trying to console Little Beaver. It was not unusual for a man to have several wives and Rain Woman was not jealous when her husband married the younger woman.

Suddenly something started to happen down in the camp. People stood up and Little Beaver could see a guard come running through the valley from the south side. The Chokonen followed him to the chief's house and she saw Nachi greet him. Were there enemies close at hand?

Little Beaver stood up too, dried her tears, and went down toward the camp. When she reached the house the others made way for her. She stopped in front of her husband and looked questioningly at him.

"Cochise, Bearfoot, and Gray Warrior have stopped hunting," said Nachi. "They are on their way back, with an old woman and a baby."

✦ Nachi

They arrived a few hours later.

Nachi stood waiting with his arms crossed. He was dressed simply. He was unarmed and wore no paint or finery. His dignity alone showed he was a chief. He was tall and powerfully built and his face had stern lines. His dark hair was streaked with gray. Nachi was no longer young.

The little procession made its way slowly down over the sandy slope at the southern end of the valley. Gray Warrior rode first, followed by Cochise and the old woman side by side. Bearfoot rode behind them. Nachi's gaze was fixed on the woman. She held a baby in her arms, just as the guard had said.

"It is Good Care," said the chief suddenly.

"Who is Good Care?" asked Little Beaver. She stood a little to the right of her husband. On his left stood Rain Woman. The other Chokonen stood on either side of them.

"She is midwife to my brother's people in the Rain Valley," replied Nachi.

The riders approached. Cochise and Good Care rode up and halted in front of the chief. Cochise jumped down from his horse and gave the reins to a boy who came running up to help. Then he went over to Good Care and took Son-of-Thunder from her. The old woman climbed down. She was stiff and weary.

"Welcome to the Chiricahua Mountains, Good Care," said Nachi.

"Thank you, Nachi."

"Why are you so far from home, and who is the child?"

"I bring grievous news," said Good Care. "Your brother is dead. We were attacked by Mexican soldiers five days ago. They killed everyone. Only your brother's newborn son and I survived. His name is Son-of-Thunder. Your brother was up in the mountains when he saw the soldiers coming. He wanted to warn us but didn't get back in time. He did not die at once and he asked me to bring the boy north to you. He said his last great wish was that you, Nachi, should bring up Son-of-Thunder as your own child."

Tears came into the chief's eyes. He stood silent for a while. Yet one more of his nearest and dearest was gone. Sorrow washed over his soul. Swift Deer had been the only one of his brothers left alive. There had been two more, but they were dead too, one of a sickness, the other in battle against the Yaqui. Swift Deer had been the youngest child of the family, and Nachi had been like a father to him.

He stretched out his arms.

"Give me Son-of-Thunder to hold," he said.

Cochise passed the little one over to him, and Nachi laid Son-of-Thunder gently in the crook of his arm. He looked at him and put a hand on his forehead.

"Is he feverish?"

"Yes," replied Good Care. "He needs rest and woman's milk."

Then Little Beaver stepped forward.

"I have milk," she said.

Nachi gave Son-of-Thunder to her, and Little Beaver held him close to her breast and went into the wickiup. Nachi looked at Good Care.

"You are in need of rest too," he said. "Rain Woman will take you to our house and look after you. But first I want to ask you something. You say the Mexicans attacked you five days ago. Why has it taken you so long to ride here?"

"For the first night and the next day your brother was still alive, and I stayed with him. Afterwards I buried him. I buried his wife also, and my son. Then I ran with Son-of-Thunder in my arms, for the Mexican soldiers had stolen all our horses. Yesterday in the south of the Blue Mountains I saw a Mexican soldier and killed him. It was his horse." ·

Nachi looked questioningly at her.

"Was he a scout?"

"No, I looked out for the others. He was alone."

"A Mexican soldier alone in the mountains?"

"Yes."

Nachi thought about it.

"Why do you think he was alone, Good Care?" he asked.

"I am not sure," answered the old woman, "but I prayed often to Usen for help. Son-of-Thunder was ill and I prayed that he might live. I believe Usen sent the soldier into the mountains because he wanted to save

Son-of-Thunder. But it puzzles me why he didn't just send a horse, without a rider."

Nachi answered at once, quietly and decisively, "Usen would not want you to have a wild horse. Usen wanted to give you a trained horse, a big strong horse. And then he wanted you to avenge the death of your son, so he had to send the Mexican soldier as well."

✦ *The Cradle*

Good Care slept for a long time. She woke up late in the day to Little Beaver's friendly smile.

"You've slept like a child, Good Care," she said.

Son-of-Thunder was at Little Beaver's breast. Good Care looked at Little Beaver with a question in her eyes.

"Yes, he is all right now," said Little Beaver, "and I am happy."

Rain Woman came in through the low door. She brought Good Care a beaker of hot soup.

"Drink this," she said. "Afterwards Nachi wants to talk to you. He is waiting outside."

Nachi sat beside the fire with a lighted cigarette in his hand, dried tobacco rolled in an oak leaf. When Good Care came out of the wickiup he greeted her and motioned for her to sit on the other side of the fireplace.

The chief was younger than Good Care, but his face was wrinkled too, and scarred from many battles. He drew at the cigarette and they sat in silence for a while. Then he began to speak.

"I have consulted the elders, Good Care, and we all agree that you are welcome to live here with us if you wish. If you have relatives you would rather go to, I and some of the braves will take you to them."

Good Care's eyes grew distant.

"The people in the Rain Valley were all Nedni,*" she said, "but most of the Nedni camps were further south, deep in the Sierra Madre Mountains. My only brother moved there too when he married. He passed away a long time ago. So did my husband. They were both killed by Mexicans. And five days ago I lost my sisters too, their children and grandchildren. And my only son was killed as well, Nachi. My family is no more."

The chief did not speak at once. He understood what Good Care had said. N'de men move to their wives' settlement when they marry; only the women go on living where they have grown up. Men of the blood leave, men of other blood come.

"Then," said Nachi, "you can build a wickiup for yourself here with us. Little Beaver will be a mother to Son-of-Thunder and I will be his father. You, Good Care, will be one of us. You will gather provisions with the other women, and Cochise and I will give you meat when we come home from the hunt. Is there anything you want to ask me?"

Good Care took thought before she answered.

"I would like Son-of-Thunder to have a good cradle," she said.

"I have already thought of that," said Nachi.

And while the birds sang and pollen scented the valley Chief Nachi went over to the neighboring camp and

*Nedni was the name of one of the N'de bands. They were also called the Southern Chiricahua Band.

asked See-in-the-Dark if he would make a cradle for Son-of-Thunder.

"Yes, I will do that with pleasure," said the old medicine man, "but first you must give me a light-colored buckskin and three more things. Give me whatever you like."

So Nachi went back and chose the finest buckskin he owned. Then he found a good bow and a leather shield he thought the medicine man would like. After that he went to the enclosure where the Chokonen kept their horses and selected one of his own, a fine strong mare he had taken from the Mexicans. The old medicine man smiled with pleasure when Nachi returned with the four gifts.

"The cradle will be ready before sunset tomorrow," he said.

And early the next day when the mountains were tinged rose-red in the morning light, See-in-the-Dark went out to find materials for the cradle. The frame would be of oak or walnut, the back of soft sotol. For the "ceiling," which would protect Son-of-Thunder from sun and rain, he would use a piece of the trunk of a red chokeberry. The cradle would not stand on the ground but hang from Little Beaver's back all day, and Son-of-Thunder would also need a foot support. For that See-in-the-Dark would use ash.

The old man spent the whole morning searching canyons and mountain ridges where he knew the different trees could be found. He did not take the first samples he came across, for a suitable cradle for Son-of-Thunder must be properly made. The cradle was a N'de's first home, and such a home must be both serviceable and beautiful.

As See-in-the-Dark looked around, he sang and prayed. He was dressed in soft, light brown moccasins, loincloth, and a long tunic of white buckskin. The tunic was decorated with painted figures representing sun and moon, stars, clouds, the rainbow, rain, and hail. On his head he wore a little leather cap with three big eagle's feathers. A painted bag hung over one shoulder. He wore jewelry and amulets and a ring in one ear. His arrows were carried in a quiver on his back and his bow over his shoulder. A sharp knife hung from his belt.

Later in the day when he returned to his wickiup and began to shape the cradle, he continued to sing and pray. He prayed that Son-of-Thunder would he happy in his cradle and that his future life would be long and rich in fortunate events.

And when darkness drifted down with its fireflies and night sounds the cradle stood finished in the wickiup. It was upholstered with leather, and the leather was newly painted with yellow ochre.

Chief Nachi had sent runners with invitations to the other settlements in the mountains, and by morning hundreds of Chokonen had gathered around the open space where the ceremony was to take place. They all knew that Nachi's brother was dead, but no one talked about it. The N'de did not like thinking about death; they preferred to celebrate life, and the cradle ceremony was not merely an act of thanksgiving for the newborn child but for everything that grows and flourishes.

See-in-the-Dark came walking slowly out into the circle. With his hand he beat a small leather drum. Behind him walked Little Beaver with Son-of-Thunder in her arms and the cradle on her back. Two of the elder braves who were also medicine men sang softly. Several of the other spectators began to join in the song.

See-in-the-Dark reached the center of the circle. The drumming and singing ceased. The old medicine man put the drum down on the ground, opened his leather bag, and took out a smaller one filled with flower pollen. Little Beaver held out Son-of-Thunder and See-in-the-Dark made four little circles of pollen on the boy's face. Then he held Son-of-Thunder out toward the directions of the four winds—first to the east, then south, then west and north. Then he did the same with the cradle.

Then See-in-the-Dark called to Good Care.

"Good Care, come forward and fasten the amulet!"

And the old midwife from the Rain Valley came into the circle and fastened the little piece of wood touched by lightning to the cradle.

See-in-the-Dark turned to Little Beaver.

"Now you can put him in the cradle," he said, and Little Beaver carefully laid her new foster son in his cradle.

"This boy will have a long life," said See-in-the-Dark in a loud voice. "Now take him with you and bring him up well."

The ceremony was over, and the feasting began with eating and drinking. Then the children played, the women sang, and the men gradually moved over to the games field to play "hoop and pole." They played for things they had with them. Bow was wagered for bow, skin for skin, even horse for horse, and the winner won not only glory but riches as well.

Later in the evening they made a great fire on the ceremony ground and then the circle dance began, in which all who wanted to could take part. Many sang and the sound of the drums echoed among the mountains.

The flames leaped and fell and when darkness covered the valley, the light of the flames shone on Good Care's old face too. The old midwife looked somber. The troubled wrinkle between her eyebrows was carved deep and while the others sang and rejoiced in the feast, Good Care's heart was filled with grief. She had brought Son-of-Thunder north to Nachi and had fastened the amulet to the cradle, but she herself had lost all her nearest and dearest, her son, her sisters, their children and grandchildren.

And during the days that followed her sorrows grew heavier. She built herself a wickiup, and Little Beaver and Rain Woman gave her utensils and helped her in many ways. Now and then she looked after Son-of-Thunder, and when Cochise and Nachi came home from hunting she had fresh meat. She went out with the other women to collect fruit, roots, nuts, berries, and leaves. But in the end her grief became too heavy for the old woman to bear and even though she worked hard she lay awake in the wickiup at night brooding. Each day she grew thinner and visibly older. A bitter line etched itself around her mouth and her expression was melancholy and remote. One morning her neighbors noticed that she had not come out of her wickiup to light her fire. Little Beaver went to see how she was and when she came out again she said quietly, "She has passed away."

Then they buried the old woman, burned her wickiup and the few small possessions she had brought with her, and never mentioned her name again. For even though she had been brave, even though she had run across the desert with Son-of-Thunder in her arms, now she was dead. And the N'de never mentioned the dead by name.

✦ *Growing Up with the Chokonen*

Nachi and Rain Woman had four children, but they were all grown up. The three daughters lived with their husbands and children, while Cochise had still not found anyone to share his life with. But he had his own wickiup.

Little Beaver nursed Son-of-Thunder, looked after him, and sang to him before he fell asleep at night. She carried him on her back in the ochre-colored cradle, and it was she who made the little moccasins he wore when he took his first hesitant steps. So even though Son-of-Thunder was the only surviving member of the people from the Rain Valley, he was not alone or lonely. Little Beaver became his new mother and Nachi his new father. Rain Woman too grew fond of him and Son-of-Thunder was happy in the wickiup with the three Chokonen.

He grew into a happy, lively boy who ran around with the other children among the wickiups in the settlement. He was never still. Now he would be up a tree, now deep down in a canyon. He often climbed around in the big boulders of a talus, and some began to call him Stone Cat. That name might have stuck, for a N'de

41

seldom kept the same name all through his life. But Nachi said that because the boy had been born in a thunderstorm and because he was the only survivor of a massacre, his name could well bring luck.

"And therefore," said the chief, "I wish him to keep the name Son-of-Thunder."

The Chokonen felt these were wise words and no one said Stone Cat any more.

Son-of-Thunder loved life. He drank from the little streams, he listened to the sounds of nature. Early in spring he watched life begin. The birds built nests, laid eggs, and hatched their young. The cows calved, the horses had foals, trees and bushes grew buds that burst into tender green leaves. In summer everything was flowering and beautiful and Son-of-Thunder savored the scent of the bright prairie blooms. Later on he could pick berries and fruit, and his mouth was constantly blue or red, until the landscape turned red-brown in autumn. At last winter's ghostly face came frowning over the mountains.

Son-of-Thunder listened to the voice of nature and he listened to Little Beaver. It was only when his beautiful gentle mother stroked his forehead and talked quietly to him that he could sit still. He would gaze at her with his great dark eyes, and he understood what she said.

"Mother Earth is our best friend, Son-of-Thunder. She gives us everything we need in life. The plants we gather, the game we hunt—all come from Mother Earth. So do we, and therefore the plants and animals are our sisters and brothers, and we must never harvest or kill more than we need."

That was how Little Beaver talked when they sat around the fireplace in the wickiup through the long winter evenings, and Son-of-Thunder learned to have respect for everything that grows and flourishes.

To begin with he spent most of his time playing. The girls had little dolls they sang to, and the boys crept on their stomachs through the grass and played hunters. Son-of-Thunder often searched for lucky four-leaved clovers, and sometimes he pinched the buds of cotton plants and used them as chewing gum. One day he and some of the other children found a beehive up in the branches of a tree. They collected twigs to make a fire under the tree and smoked out the bees. Then they treated themselves to the luscious honey.

When Son-of-Thunder was six years old Nachi gave him a little bow and arrows. He learned to bend the bow, send off the arrow, and hit what he was aiming at.

"Father, come and see! I hit it, I hit it!" he shouted.

"Yes, I can see that," said Nachi, "but it's best to let others praise your feats. You must never boast of them yourself. If you have self-respect you don't need to boast."

"I wasn't boasting, I was just pleased I hit it," thought Son-of-Thunder, but said nothing. And later on, when he and the other boys had shooting competitions, he made no comment if he was the winner.

Son-of-Thunder and the Chokonen lived in a land of desert and plains broken up by mountain chains that ran north-south, up to fifty kilometers long and high enough for the snow to cover some of them in winter. Between the huge peaks were thick forests, deep ravines, and hidden valleys. Those were the sorts of sites the Chokonen chose for their camps.

The band did not all live together in one place but split into smaller groups. Groups of braves from these settlements often went out hunting together, or rode off on raids or battles against a hostile band. A raid was for plunder and the braves stole the enemy's goods, generally at dawn when he was asleep. The battles were campaigns of revenge and then the Chokonen went out to kill. When the enemy was numerous and strong the whole band gathered for war and Nachi led them.

As a boy Son-of-Thunder often looked on when the men prepared themselves for war. They painted their faces and he heard them singing and dancing around the fires the night before they set off. The lead singer was called Pathfinder. He was younger than See-in-the-Dark but had been given knowledge of enemies and war by the gods. Son-of-Thunder lay in the dark wickiup and he thought Pathfinder's song was fearsome. It had a strange alien tone.

"One day I will be a warrior too," thought Son-of-Thunder, "but that won't be for a long time yet."

For he knew that death lay in wait in battle, and some of the men who rode out would never come home again. He had been a witness to that several times, and the widows and children of the dead went around the wickiups weeping. Son-of-Thunder put his fingers in his ears and tried not to think of war and Pathfinder's song.

The time came when Nachi went off to raid or fight more and more rarely. The Chokonen still sought his advice on everyday matters or asked him to settle disputes between neighbors, but the years had piled upon him and his body no longer obeyed his will. Little by little Cochise took over his place in the fight against the Mexicans and hostile Indian bands.

"We Chokonen hate and despise the Mexicans," Cochise said to Son-of-Thunder, "but the Pima and the Yaqui are our enemies too. You must learn to scorn them as well, for they are as cowardly as coyote."

The winter when Son-of-Thunder turned seven years old Nachi fell seriously ill. The Chokonen had moved westward over to the Dragoon Mountains where the valleys were free of snow. Nachi lay wasted and burning with fever in his wickiup, and Rain Woman and Little Beaver looked after him as best they could. Several medicine men were sent for. They gave him herbal drinks and rubbed him with salves. They sang and prayed for him, but Nachi's life was beyond saving, and in the early spring he died. He was buried in a grotto, and Son-of-Thunder cried for several days. In the time that followed he stayed by himself, silent and sorrowful.

In the east the snow was melting in the Chiricahua Mountains. The rivers and streams ran free and the birds practiced their spring songs. The Chokonen returned to their favorite camping grounds, but Son-of-Thunder took no joy in the new life and all that was happening.

Then one day Cochise went up to him and said, "Come with me, Son-of-Thunder. We'll go for a walk together. There's something I want to tell you."

Son-of-Thunder stood up unwillingly and went with his brother. They went out of the camp, up through the forests and far up into the mountains to a summit with a view in all directions. They could see for a great distance, over deserts and plains to other forests and mountains. Son-of-Thunder looked at his brother with a question in his big sorrowful eyes.

"We have told you before that you were born far away to the south," said Cochise, "and you know the Mexican soldiers murdered all the Nedni who lived in the Rain Valley. You were only a few days old when you came to us, and once, when you asked me, I told you that an old woman brought you here to the north. That was true, and you have lived with us since then, Son-of-Thunder. Little Beaver became your mother, he who has now passed on became your father, and I became your brother. We grew to love you and I know you came to love us too. And that is good."

Cochise fell silent. His gaze grew distant and he gave long thought to what he was about to say. He dreaded mentioning the dead by name, but the time had come for it. He turned to his little brother again, and Son-of-Thunder met his eyes as he had learned to do.

"When someone talks to you, you must look him straight in the eyes," Nachi had said. "Only when you feel scorn and disgust should you look away, but never bow your head. Then you yourself will be scorned and despised."

"Your first father was called Swift Deer," said Cochise. "His name must never be spoken again, but he was given it because he was the best runner among the Chokonen. When he met your mother, who was a Nedni, he moved south to the Rain Valley. She was called Little Eagle because she was born in the season when the first fledglings come into the world. Her name must never be spoken again either.

"On the first day of your life your father went up into the mountains and found the amulet you are wearing now in a thong around your neck. It was to bring you luck, and it has done so.

"Afterwards he sat down on a mountaintop like this one. Before he died he told the old woman he had pictured taking you up there when you grew older. He wanted to show you how beautiful our country is.

"It was then he suddenly saw the Mexican soldiers approaching, and he ran and ran to get down to the Rain Valley and warn the others. All the time he was running he thought of you and your first mother. But he only managed to save you."

Cochise paused once more. His gaze grew distant again. His words had sunk deep into Son-of-Thunder's heart. Now he knew the names of his first parents and he felt he had suddenly come close to them. And what Cochise had said was not terrible. His brother's voice had been kind and calm. It did not remind him in the least of Pathfinder's song before battle.

"All you can see from here is Chokonen land, Son-of-Thunder," Cochise went on. "Not only the N'de grow up in this land, but birds too, big animals and small, the elk and the cricket, trees, bushes, and flowers. The grass blades bend before the wind out there and everything is alive. That is how Usen has arranged the world.

"But everything that lives must die some time, and we Chokonen fear death. The one who is killed at night must spend eternity wandering in the dark, and the ghostly bodies of the dead can plague enemies and foes who are still alive.

"But the good N'de who die in the daytime are allowed to live on in another country, a green and fertile land far down under the earth. That land is even more beautiful than ours. There is game in abundance and the braves who go there win great victories over their enemies.

"Both your fathers are in that country now, Son-of-Thunder," Cochise finished his talk. "And so you must not grieve for them anymore. Your first mother is there too, and she is happy."

That night Son-of-Thunder slept soundly, and in a dream he saw a great green landscape with shady woods and grazing flocks of deer. He saw Nachi smile, and he saw Swift Deer running like an antelope over the plains. Later on in his dream he saw a woman too, and the two men called her Little Eagle. She had big dark eyes. All three were sitting around a fire roasting a deer's calf. They were laughing, and then Son-of-Thunder laughed with them.

"You were laughing so heartily in your sleep," Little Beaver said when he woke up.

Son-of-Thunder smiled at her for the first time in many days, and then he told her of his dream. Little Beaver sat looking at him for a long time.

"That was a good dream you had last night, Son-of-Thunder," she said. "Now we can feel at peace, for they are in a happy place."

Cochise became the new chief of the Chokonen. He led the braves on raids and in battle from victory to victory, and they came home with cattle, horses, and gifts for all.

But all the same the new chief was worried, for the white eyes pushed into the N'de lands in ever greater numbers, and one day in autumn one of the guards rode into the camp and reported a large army of white eyes with blue tunics, fire-weapons, and long knives. Cochise climbed up to a lookout point in the mountains and studied the large army from a distance. The soldiers were mounted on powerful horses, and the desert dust rose high in the air. Then Cochise remembered something he had heard about bloody battles between the Mexicans and the white eyes further east. The Mexicans had been defeated, and the chief looked at the long column of mounted men disappearing toward the west and felt sorely troubled about the future.

Early the next spring there came an unexpected visit from the northeast and soon everyone in the Chiricahua Mountains knew that Chief Red Sleeves was on his way with a small company. He was coming to talk with Cochise.

No N'de chief had such renown as had Red Sleeves. He was wise and knew much, and at one time his name had been He-Who-Sits-and-Thinks. He was invincible in hand-to-hand combat and he had led Bedonkohe and Chihenne* to great victories over Mexican and Comanche. He was rich as well, with three wives and many children. One of his daughters was called Ear-of-Corn, a lovely young woman who had come with him now.

"Welcome, Red Sleeves," said Cochise and held out his hands.

Red Sleeves jumped down from his horse and came toward him smiling. Cochise was tall and strong, but the Bedonkohe chief was taller and stronger. The two men held each other's hands.

*Bedonkohe and Chihenne are the names of the two N'de bands. Some have considered them as one band, known as the Eastern Chiricahua Band.

"It is good to see a youth who is strong and wise," said Red Sleeves.

"It is even better to see an older man with greater strength and wisdom," said Cochise.

Small groups of Chokonen from other settlements came running to meet the chief, who had many friends and relations in the Chiricahua Mountains. That night there was a great festival with fires and circle-dancing. Ear-of-Corn sat with the other women and sang.

"I saw an army of white eyes with blue tunics when the earth was red-brown," said Cochise. "They were as many as the sunrises from ghost face to ghost face.[†] They came from the east and disappeared toward the west."

"I have met them," said Red Sleeves, "and I spoke with their chief. His name is General Kearny and he is very powerful. We met him by the old mines in Santa Rita del Cobre before he rode westward. He was going to fight the Mexicans and I offered him aid. The N'de know these lands, I said, let us defeat the Mexicans once and for all. He refused the offer but asked us for strong mules. We supplied him, then he left."

Cochise frowned.

"Why did he refuse?"

"I don't know. The white eyes are not like us. Now they say the Mexicans are no longer lords of Bedonkohe and Chihenne lands. They say the lands belong to the white eyes."

Cochise snorted.

"N'de country has never belonged to the Mexicans. The Mexican frontiers exist only on papers they call maps. I cannot see any frontiers here in the mountains or out on the plains. Not in the past, and not now."

[†]Ghost face was the N'de expression for winter.

"Nor do I see any frontiers," said Red Sleeves. "The white eyes' frontiers are found only on maps also. The white eyes' papers cannot take the land Usen gave us away from us."

Red Sleeves picked a twig from one of the fires and lit himself a cigarette with the glowing end.

"I have brought my youngest daughter with me," he said, "her name is Ear-of-Corn and she is a daughter of Ana."

"Yes, I have seen her," said Cochise. "She is beautiful, and I hear she is wise too."

"There are many who would like her for a wife," said Red Sleeves. "The Bedonkohe and the Chokonen have lived in peace and as good friends for a long time. I would not object to my daughter moving here if the right brave wanted her."

A small smile curved Cochise's lips, but when he spoke he was serious.

"It is better for others to speak of my feats, but Ear-of-Corn will be treated well if she comes to live in my wickiup."

Red Sleeves was a guest in the Chiricahua Mountains for four days. When he left, Cochise and Ear-of-Corn stood side by side watching his little company ride away, for Red Sleeves had said that Ear-of-Corn could stay and live with the Chokonen.

"If Cochise leaves, the Chokonen will lose their chief, but if Ear-of-Corn stays, I have a daughter in the Chiricahua Mountains."

Son-of-Thunder grew older, and he listened and learned. During the warm summer evenings he heard the grown-ups talking around the fires of raids and battles and far-off places. And in the winter when the N'de shel-tered from the weather in their wickiups, Son-of-Thunder drank in all the strange tales and myths of giants and gods. He learned about the greatest and mightiest of them all, Usen, who had created all life. He learned about the White Painted Woman and about the Child of the Water. Some of the older people said those two were siblings; others thought they were mother and son. He was also told the stories about the sly and cunning Coyote, about the Mountain People and the Thunder People.

His favorite was the tale of the Thunder People, gi-ants who had lived on earth a long time ago and taught the N'de how to hunt. But the N'de had forgotten to thank them, so the Thunder People had found a new home for themselves in the clouds. They still went hunt-ing and they almost always hit what they aimed at. The lightning was the flash of the Thunder People's arrows, and the N'de always tried to hide themselves when the thunderstorms swept over the land.

But Son-of-Thunder wasn't afraid of the lightning. He knew he had been born on a night of thunder and that was why he had been given his name. Nachi had said the name had brought him luck, for he was the only survivor from the Rain Valley.

One night when the lightning flashed he crept out of the wickiup. Little Beaver and Rain Woman begged him to stay, but he took no notice of them. When he stood among the wickiups and saw the blue flashes ripping through the skies he was not in the least afraid. He felt a strange kinship with the invisible beings up there in the sky.

The Mountain People were gods who lived deep in-side the hills behind great doors. They were numerous and powerful and ruthless toward their enemies. Son-of-Thunder felt close to them as well. When the young N'de girls were ready to be initiated as women there was a great ceremony, in which the medicine man joined with four dancers dressed as Mountain People dancers. They wore masks, but they did not frighten Son-of-Thunder either.

"When I grow up I would like to be a dancer myself," he thought.

And he gradually came to realize that everything to do with the ceremonies and the gods meant more to him than to others of his age. Sometimes he could sit for days pondering on things that were mysterious and inexplicable.

Ear-of-Corn had children and that gave Cochise even more mouths to feed, for the chief did not hunt only for his own family. He also provided game for Son-of-Thunder, Little Beaver, and Rain Woman, and the time came when Son-of-Thunder was allowed to go out hunting with him. Little by little he became a hunter.

One day Cochise said, "Soon you will be a warrior, Son-of-Thunder, but first you must learn to run, even faster than you do now. We Chokonen are few but our enemies are many. Up to now we have fought against the Pima, the Yaqui, and the Mexicans, but more and more white eyes are marching into N'de country. One day we may have to fight them too.

"Because there are so few of us we must be more cunning than our enemies. We must lure them into ambushes, attack when they least expect it, and withdraw swiftly. So you must run faster, much faster."

The next day Cochise took Son-of-Thunder with him to the edge of the desert and pointed to a mountain far away in the heat haze.

"Your feet must be your best friends," he said. "You must always be able to rely on your feet. More than you rely on Little Beaver and me. Run to that mountain over there. Do not stop to drink from the spring, just turn around and run back again at once. I will wait for you here in the shade."

Son-of-Thunder did as Cochise bid him. He ran and ran under the burning sun. The heat was terrible and the mountain was far, far away. He ran the whole day, and when the western sky was a deep red he came staggering toward the place where Cochise sat. His eyes were glazed, his lips cracked.

"Drink," said Cochise and passed him a water bag.

Another time when they were up in the mountains Cochise showed him a huge strong oak tree.

"The enemy is strong, his muscles are hard, and he does not breathe heavily when he fights. You, Son-of-Thunder, must be stronger. Fight that tree over there."

So Son-of-Thunder went for the stout oak trunk with clenched fists. He hit and hit until his knuckles bled.

"Harder!" shouted Cochise. "Hit harder! Push the tree over!"

And Son-of-Thunder kept on. He punched and kicked until his whole body hurt. He tried to get his arms around the tree, tried to pull it down, tear it up by the roots. In the end he collapsed on the grass, totally exhausted. Cochise came up to him.

"Get up!" he snarled at him. "The enemy will kill you! Do you hear? Get up!"

With an effort Son-of-Thunder managed to lift his head from the grass.

"Get up!" repeated Cochise.

Son-of-Thunder pushed on his hands and slowly got to his knees. The earth went around and around. He fell back, and Cochise shouted at him again.

"Get up! The enemy will kill you!"

But Son-of-Thunder lay still. Then Cochise kicked him hard on the thigh.

"Can't you hear what I say, boy?" he yelled. "You must get up!"

With the last of his strength Son-of-Thunder crawled on all fours up to the oak tree. His fingers clutched at the trunk, his nails dug into the bark, and slowly he hauled his body off the ground. Finally he was standing up.

"Good," breathed Cochise. "Now we can go home."

Then Son-of-Thunder staggered back to camp at the heels of his chief.

That night he could not sleep. He lay in the wickiup fighting against the pain and the tears.

"Why does it have to be like that?" he thought. "Why can't we find a country no enemies know about? A valley full of game, with deep woodlands, cool springs, and peaceful plains, far away from Mexicans, Yaqui, and white eyes. I don't want to be a warrior. I want to be a dancer!"

But in the morning Cochise came to see how he was. Little Beaver and Rain Woman went out. Little Beaver had put salve on Son-of-Thunder's sore hands and leaves on his swollen knuckles.

Cochise squatted down beside Son-of-Thunder.

"Did you sleep?" he asked.

"No."

"The pains will die down," said Cochise. "Rest for a day or two. But now the time has come for you to come with us on raids and warfare. The first four raids you will be given simple tasks. But then, the fifth time, you must go into battle, and then you must fight with the leaders."

Son-of-Thunder looked at his brother.

"Do you really think it is time after what you saw yesterday?"

Cochise smiled.

"You fought like a mountain lion," he said.

"Oh, yes," said Son-of-Thunder, "and was beaten by a tree."

Cochise grew serious.

"Listen to me," he said. "You can tell the birds by their song. You can find a trail, follow it, and bring down a deer with the first arrow. You ride with the best, you clamp yourself to the horse just like a bat does to a tree. And yesterday you fought like a mountain lion, you certainly did, and the big oak wept."

Son-of-Thunder looked at Cochise. He knew his brother spoke the truth. He knew it was time.

"I have spoken with See-in-the-Dark," said Cochise. "He is very old now, but his mind is clear. When you are better we will go to see him, so that we can pray for you and give you good advice and prepare you for the four raids."

"There is a peculiar sweetish smell in the dimness of the medicine man's wickiup," thought Son-of-Thunder. On the floor, which was covered with skins, were pots and baskets filled with salves and herbs, skeletons of small animals, and cooking utensils. Drums and shields hung from ceiling and walls, eagle's feathers, "singing" wooden objects, medicine crosses, medicine hats, and bags filled with sacred things. There were white buckskin tunics with painted symbols, hundreds of amulets, and colored ribbons to which were fastened pieces of wood, shells, mountain crystals, feathers, and claws.

See-in-the-Dark himself sat leaning against the wall, supported by big leather cushions. His face was like a dried-up bog, but his eyes shone clear among all the wrinkles. When he spoke his voice was faint and hoarse.

"It is good to see you, Son-of-Thunder," he said. "You have your family's face, you are pleasing, and you are strong. I have lived for many summers now. Soon I will go to the green country where the N'de hunt eternally. There I will sing and pray and conduct great ceremonies. But first we two will spend a few days here in my wickiup. Do you feel ready to be a warrior now?"

Son-of-Thunder was slow to reply.

"Yes, I suppose I do," he said.

The old medicine man frowned. He had seen Son-of-Thunder hesitate, and his reply had not been firm and decided enough.

"Are you not sure?" asked See-in-the-Dark.

Son-of-Thunder thought it over. He wanted to say what he felt to See-in-the-Dark.

"Yes, I know the time has come. I feel ready for it, and Cochise has taught me much. It is just that I am looking forward more to the day when I can become a dancer than to the day when I become a warrior."

See-in-the-Dark sat for a long time in silence, but when he spoke again a new warmth had come into his voice.

"I wanted to be a dancer as well when I was young," he began, "and I know many other medicine men have felt the same. We felt ourselves drawn to the unknown, to the rituals and the ceremonies. The gods knew about this, so they made us medicine men. They showed themselves to us in dreams, or they gave us signs when we were alone. They taught us to heal, they taught us the sacred ceremonies, and there were some who learned how to lead the N'de into victory over their enemy through prayer and good advice. But first, Son-of-Thunder, we all had to become warriors, we all had to fight, for the N'de are few. All of us had to learn to be cunning first, for the enemy are many. The best medicine men were all good warriors. They knew something about this life. So they had to learn something about the other as well. I will give you a song, Son-of-Thunder. Pass me that drum."

Son-of-Thunder passed him the drum and this is the song See-in-the-Dark sang to him in the wickiup:

> *"You, son of the Thunder People in the clouds.*
> *You, son of the Thunder People in the clouds.*
> *It is better to have lightning in the hand than*
> *thunder in the mouth.*
> *It is better to have lightning in the hand than*
> *thunder in the mouth."*

Then Son-of-Thunder stayed for four days and nights with the old medicine man who had long ago been the head of his cradle ceremony. He learned much that helped him later, and which even saved his life several times in battle against his enemies.

✦ *The Four Raids*

The white eyes who had infiltrated N'de country were not trappers. In the northern and eastern regions gold diggers roamed the mountains in search of the shining metal, and the soldiers in blue tunics had built fortresses out of heavy logs beside the rivers Gila and Rio Grande. Farmers put up barns and corrals for horses and cattle and plowed long furrows in the earth. Gradually they encroached on the hunting grounds of the Bedonkohe and Chihenne.

The Chokonen began to notice the presence of the white eyes as well. Great wagon trains rolled across the plains toward the west, and Tucson, which had once been a Mexican settlement, now became a town full of white eyes. And at Calabasas southwest of the Dragoon mountains the soldiers took over and called the place Fort Buchanan.

Now and then the Chokonen stole a few horses and cattle from gold diggers and farmers, but Cochise asked the braves to avoid trouble with the blue tunics. The Chokonen were still lords of the Dragoon and Chiricahua Mountains, but the chief looked on with misgiving as the hairy men from the east steadily increased in numbers. If they did not go away again but continued to settle in N'de country, war was inevitable.

But the Mexicans were still the Chokonen's arch enemies and the braves went raiding deep into Mexico. One day Son-of-Thunder asked to go with them.

The first raid took place in late summer, and seven braves set off, six warriors and Son-of-Thunder. He rode a brown mare that belonged to Cochise, the one he usually borrowed when they went hunting. For several days he went along with the others southwest in the Sonora region. Their goal was a new Mexican settlement, and in the gray dawn while the warriors crawled through the grass toward barns and corrals Son-of-Thunder stood in a wood guarding the horses. Before the Mexicans had left their beds that morning their horses and mules were on their way northward with the Chokonen. Son-of-Thunder had felt nervous alone in the wood, but in the evening he rejoiced in the triumph and was present when the booty was shared out. And the next time he rode out he was on his own horse. It was black with big white patches.

The second raid was in the autumn, but although more braves took part, this time they returned empty-handed. They were again out to steal horses from a farm in Sonora, but the Mexicans had placed guards, and the warriors were spotted. One was wounded when the Mexicans opened fire and the Chokonen made for home. Son-of-Thunder had again been put in charge of the horses but had been in no danger. All the same his heart beat faster and fear crawled like a cold snake over his back when the shots sounded from the farm.

Early the next spring while the Chokonen were still encamped in the Dragoon Mountains he went out on his third raid. They were on their way to a small mining town in the south of the Chihuahua region when they caught sight of four Mexican mule traders, who had caught a large herd of mules and were driving them westward toward the town of Casas Grandes. Cochise himself led the braves and for two days they concealed themselves and followed the Mexicans and the mules at a distance. On the third day the Mexicans had to traverse a long, narrow pass. Cochise ordered three of the braves, who all carried firearms, to ride ahead and position themselves in the middle of the pass. When the mule traders approached the three warriors opened fire. While the Mexicans tried to take cover from the bullets the mules turned around and rushed back along the pass to where the other Chokonen lay in wait. In a couple of minutes the mules had changed owners.

The Chokonen followed the seasons and the migrating game and once more traveled eastward. They found their old camping sites untouched, and Son-of-Thunder felt light at heart. There was nowhere he liked to be so much as here in the Chiricahua Mountains, and he felt eager to go searching for four-leaved clovers as he had when he was younger. But the clovers had to wait, for Cochise wanted him to go hunting. When after a few days they returned with fresh meat, Little Beaver had built a wickiup for Son-of-Thunder. Rain Woman had said that it was time for him to live on his own and not share a house with old women.

That spring Red Sleeves rode into the Chiricahua Mountains with the whole of the Bedonkohe band. They brought all their belongings with them, many horses and many mules.

"Many white eyes have spread over our land, and we have decided to come south for a time," said Red Sleeves. "We know a good safe place in the mountains, and we have made a peace treaty with the Mexicans in the town of Kaskiyeh, the one they call Janos. We are going to hunt and trade with the Mexicans, and in the autumn we will go north again."

The Bedonkohe stayed in the Chiricahua Mountains for a week and Red Sleeves had long talks with Cochise, Ear-of-Corn, and his grandchild. Some of his other Chokonen relatives came to greet the chief. The two tribes lived together in friendship, and Son-of-Thunder met young people he had never spoken to before. One was called Eagle's Claw and he, like Son-of-Thunder, was soon to be a warrior. They described the raids they had been on to each other, and they ran races and had shooting competitions.

Son-of-Thunder was particularly struck by one of the braves in Red Sleeves's band. He had a young and beautiful wife and three small children. He laughed a lot but, despite this, his face had a hard look. His mouth was set in a narrow line, almost without lips.

"Who is that brave?" asked Son-of-Thunder.

"That is Go-Yak-Klah (The-One-Who-Yawns)," replied Eagle's Claw.

"That's a strange name," said Son-of-Thunder.

"Not really," said Eagle's Claw. "He got it because he slept such a lot when he was younger. I expect he'll get a new name soon."

Red Sleeves and his people soon struck camp and moved on southward and life went on as usual in the Chiricahua Mountains. But then one day a lookout came into the settlement and reported that five white eyes were making their way into the mountains some way off to the north.

"They have seven mules and many fire-weapons. They have tools as well and I think they are gold diggers," said the lookout.

Then Cochise was angry.

"Up till now the white eyes have kept out of the Chiricahua Mountains," he said, "and that is how it is going to be as long as I am alive. Fetch your weapons, braves!"

"Death to the white eyes!" someone yelled.

"No, we will let them live," said Cochise firmly, "but we will take everything they own away from them. Their trousers as well."

Then the Chokonen laughed, for everyone knew that the worst thing that could happen to the white eyes was to be left without their trousers.

As this was not to be a battle, but a raid, Son-of-Thunder asked to go along.

"Yes, you can come, but look out for yourself," said Cochise. "The white eyes are bigger and stronger than the Mexicans, and better shots."

Then the chief and all his braves ran into the mountains in a long line, for horses were merely a hindrance in this terrain. Later on in the afternoon they came in sight of the gold diggers who had pitched camp in a thicket down in a valley bottom. The gold diggers were drinking from a bottle they passed from man to man, and before the sun went down they were all asleep. Then the braves crept up to the thicket, threw themselves on the sleepers, and put their hands over their mouths. The white eyes woke up and their eyes shone with terror. But the braves remembered Cochise's command, and they were allowed to live.

Before the white eyes were sent packing they were undressed. Son-of-Thunder had never seen white eyes at such close quarters before. He thought they were incredibly ugly with their faces covered with hair, and they smelled like a foul water hole. But when he caught sight of their pink woollen underwear, and then their chalk-white bodies, he laughed till the tears came into his eyes, and his laughter infected the others. They slapped their thighs and laughed and laughed. . . . Never before had they seen anything so comical.

When at last the laughter died down Cochise talked to the white eyes in the Mexican tongue.

"Can any of you speak Spanish?" he asked.

One of the white eyes nodded.

"Yes, a little," he answered.

Cochise pointed to the east.

"Go back there where you came from," he said. "Tell the other white eyes you meet that these mountains belong to the Chokonen. Say that Cochise and his people are lords here."

"Are you Cochise?" asked the white eye.

"Yes."

"We have heard of you. Why don't you kill us?"

"Because I wish to live in peace with all white eyes," replied Cochise, "but no one must ever try to force their way into these mountains again."

"We thought you lived in the Dragoon Mountains," said the white eye.

"There. And here. Our people have lived in these mountains for many generations."

The sun went down and it began to get dark. The warriors led the five white eyes eastward through the mountains and down toward the desert.

"Go now," said Cochise.

So the naked fellows trudged off into the desert. The braves sat and watched them until they vanished into the night.

When the Chokonen returned to the camp the next day, they shared out everything they had taken from the gold diggers, and the warriors agreed that Son-of-Thunder should have one of the fire-weapons. He had coped well with the four raids and everyone had enjoyed his hearty laughter over the trouserless white eyes. Son-of-Thunder gave thanks for the weapon and went off with it to his wickiup. He sat down and cautiously ran his fingers over the barrel and stock of the old flintlock. It was heavy to carry and he knew it kicked hard when fired. More and more Chokonen had firearms by now, but bullets and powder were scarce.

That afternoon, while Son-of-Thunder still sat outside his wickiup studying the fire-weapon, Cochise came to visit.

"Be seated, Brother," said Son-of-Thunder, and the chief sat down beside him.

"Come over to me tomorrow," said Cochise, "and we will go off somewhere where you can try out your new weapon. I will show you how to use it. But remember that even if the weapon can kill at a great distance, it makes a very loud noise and the enemy can hear it a long way away. No one can hear the arrow, the battle-club and the knife, and we Chokonen fight best when we are swift and soundless."

"I will remember that," said Son-of-Thunder.

They sat for a while in silence.

Then Cochise said, "Now you will soon be a warrior, Son-of-Thunder."

"Yes."

"The next time we go out to do battle you must fight among the leaders."

"Yes, I know," said Son-of-Thunder. "But I hope it won't be for a long time," he thought to himself.

But it was not to be so very long. For while Son-of-Thunder and Cochise sat peacefully talking in the Chiricahua Mountains, another brave was standing with tears in his eyes, far to the south in Mexico, in the mountains north of Janos. He stood by himself with bowed head under a tree. Behind him, in a clearing in the forest, other N'de moved among the mutilated bodies of their relatives, friends, wives, and children. They had all lost some of their nearest and dearest, but the weeping brave had lost all—his old mother, his young wife, and his three small children.

✦ Part II: Arizpe

✦ Go-Yak-Klah
The-One-Who-Yawns

The eagle came gliding out of the south, high above the desert sands. Son-of-Thunder sat on a ledge up on the mountainside and followed it with his eyes. Now and then the great bird flapped its powerful wings a few times. Then it glided on.

It was early in the day. The August breeze lightly brushed the Chiricahua Mountains. Fruit was beginning to ripen among the branches in the fertile hidden valleys, and the air was thick with pollen. Son-of-Thunder sat in the shadow of the mountainside. Beneath him the desert stretched out toward the east. Scattered summer clouds sailed gently across the sky, and he enjoyed his post as lookout on a day like this.

Suddenly the eagle jerked in its flight, changed direction, and swung into a circling movement over the undulating sands. It cocked its head; it had caught sight of something out there. Son-of-Thunder stood up and peered into the distance. Far away to the east in the desert a rider slowly came into view over a sand dune.

The ledge was on the south side of a narrow pass, high above the entrance to the Chiricahua Mountains'

labyrinth of valleys and canyons. On the north side of the pass too there was a ledge on the mountainside and there stood another lookout searching the horizon. He was called Hare's Trail, and Son-of-Thunder could see him clearly. Hare's Trail had caught sight of the rider too.

The stranger rode forward at a steady trot which did not send the sand flying. He held his course straight for the pass and soon the two lookouts recognized him as a N'de. He was dressed as they were, and wore a head-band and long hair. Since he was coming from the east he was most likely a Bedonkohe or a Chihenne.

Hare's Trail gave a cry like a river hawk and Son-of-Thunder turned around to look at him. The distance from ledge to ledge was less than 150 meters.

First Hare's Trail pointed at himself, looking back toward the mountains. Son-of-Thunder understood what he meant and waved back at him. Then a moment later Hare's Trail had vanished. In an hour or two Cochise and the others would know the stranger was on his way. They would send out braves to meet him. Son-of-Thunder himself would be relieved of his vigil when the sun began to sink, for this was his fourth day on the ledge.

The stranger came steadily nearer, but Son-of-Thunder did not attempt to hide. He stood upright in full view of the rider. In his right hand Son-of-Thunder held his fire-weapon. His bow was over his shoulder and his quiver on his back. His knife and battle club hung from his belt.

When the rider came to the entrance to the pass he stopped his horse, lifted his head, looked up at Son-of-Thunder and made the sign of peace. He was near enough for Son-of-Thunder to be able to see his face quite clearly. It was hard and expressionless. The mouth was almost lipless, a long narrow strip above the powerful jaw, and Son-of-Thunder recognized him at once. It was the brave he had noticed when Red Sleeves and his band visited the Chiricahua Mountains on their way south.

Then he had been a stranger, but now all the N'de knew who he was. For when the Mexican soldiers had last attacked the Bedonkohe camp in the mountains north of Janos, it was he who had lost all his next of kin, his mother, his wife, and his three small children.

The brave was Go-Yak-Klah, The-One-Who-Yawns.

✦ The Council Meeting

The night had passed. The owls fell silent, the fireflies' torches died out, and the sun cast its rosy morning light over the eastern sky.

The braves sat in rows on the council meeting ground, the eldest in front, the youngest at the back. The meeting ground was on a slight slope and Son-of-Thunder could see Cochise's broad back. The-One-Who-Yawns sat beside the chief. The two men shared a cigarette and blew out the smoke into the cool morning air. The warriors sat quietly, waiting. They all knew what was going to happen, but no one knew the words to be spoken, and the gathering was tense.

Cochise made a sign, and The-One-Who-Yawns stood up and walked forward so all could see him. Once more Son-of-Thunder was struck by his features, how the whole man seemed to be carved out of the mountain.

"Chokonen," The-One-Who-Yawns began, "I stand here because my chief, Red Sleeves, and the Bedonkohe have sent me. I have a question for you, and when the answer is known I will move on south to our friends, the Nedni, in the Sierra Madre mountains, and Chief Juh. I will ask the same question there."

His words came slowly but with great strength. There was fervor and intensity in the calm speech of the Bedonkohe, and Son-of-Thunder listened.

"You have all heard what happened at Janos," continued The-One-Who-Yawns. "We had made an agreement with the Mexicans in the town. We traded peacefully with them. We walked among their houses and smoked with them in the plaza, and we left our old people, our women and children with a few warriors up in the mountains where we had pitched camp. We did not expect enemies."

The warriors nodded. They all knew the story. The Bedonkohe had gone on a peaceful mission; they were smoking in the plaza of Janos.

The-One-Who-Yawns raised his voice, "But then the Mexican mounted soldiers came from the town of Arizpe. They stabbed our women with their long knives. They stopped our children's hearts with their fire-weapons. Since then the Bedonkohe have been crushed with sorrow, but now our hearts are calling for revenge!"

The sun came over the mountain tops. Go-Yak-Klah's eyes shone like burning coals and his voice was full of hate.

"Chokonen, you are the Bedonkohe's friends. We share the same blood and I see uncles and cousins in this council gathering. The Mexicans are men, but we are men too. There are many of them, but there are many of us as well, if we join together. Then we can do to them what they have done to us. Let us hunt them down, attack them in the town where they live. I will fight among the foremost. I beg you to avenge this wrong. Are you with us? Are you with us?"

One of the warriors shouted, "Yes, I am with you!"

"Remember the rule of war: some of us will return, but some may be killed," said The-One-Who-Yawns. "Should any of you fall, no one must blame me, for you have made your own choice. And if I should die, no one must weep for me. All my dear ones were murdered there in the southern mountains, and I am ready to give my life as well if need be."

Son-of-Thunder heard every word and now he felt how those words touched something deep inside him, something that had always been there ever since Cochise had taken him up to the mountaintop and told him how his first father had run and run to save the people in the Rain Valley.

"That time it was I who lost my dear ones," thought Son-of-Thunder. "That time it was my nearest and dearest who were left lying in the blood-stained grass."

And the Bedonkohe's speech set words to Son-of-Thunder's own feelings, nourished his own anger and desire for revenge.

"Yes, we are with you!" yelled Son-of-Thunder. "Yes, we too are for war! War!"

"War!" shouted the warriors around him.

"War! War! War!"

✦ The Furious Dance

The-One-Who-Yawns took his leave of the Chokonen and went on a long way south. In a secret place deep in the Sierra Madre Mountains he met the Nedni and Chief Juh, and many volunteered to join the Bedonkohe in battle to avenge their dead.

That autumn the three bands met in the mountains where the white eyes and the Mexicans had drawn up their invisible frontiers. Sweet red algerita berries shone among yellow-brown leaves, and up on the mountain slopes were tempting black juniper berries with their bitter taste.

Son-of-Thunder had never seen so many N'de gathered in one place before, never heard so many voices, so much laughter and children crying. He was thrilled with all the new faces and enjoyed meeting Eagle's Claw again. The young Bedonkohe was a warrior now and the two had many things to talk about.

Nor had Son-of-Thunder seen Juh before, the strong, jovial chief from the Sierra Madre mountains. He may not have had as much dignity as Cochise and Red Sleeves, but he was loved by his people and hated by the Mexicans. People said that the deep valleys in the interior of the Sierra Madre Mountains were Juh's private fortress, and no Mexican officer had ever dared to lead his soldiers against those defenses. Son-of-Thunder noticed that Juh spent much time with The-One-Who-Yawns, and Eagle's Claw told him the two of them were cousins. Their fathers were brothers, but the father of The-One-Who-Yawns had gone north with his wife to Gila and become a Bedonkohe.

The three chiefs summoned the warriors to a council meeting, and as Son-of-Thunder had accomplished his four raids, he was allowed to take part. At this meeting they fixed on a safe place in the mountains where they would leave the women, children, and old people. Twenty warriors volunteered to stay and look after them.

After a few days they all set off for the appointed campsite. They put up their tepees, tents made of skins and poles, that were their homes for shorter periods.

On the night before the warriors were to leave, all the N'de gathered in a wide circle around a great fire. The moon was full and the stars sparkled; the red-gold flames flickered in the blue night. Some of the braves beat rhythmically on big leather drums, and Pathfinder started singing. Soon other voices joined in.

Son-of-Thunder knew what would happen next, and after a while he caught sight of four dancers approaching the fire from the east. They moved slowly forward, stamping their feet and swaying their bodies. Once again Son-of-Thunder felt himself drawn strongly to the dance.

"But first, Son-of-Thunder, we all had to become warriors . . ." echoed the words of See-in-the-Dark, and Son-of-Thunder knew that now the time had come when he himself must say yes or no to war. When The-One-

Who-Yawns had talked to the Chokonen in the Chiricahua Mountains a month ago, Son-of-Thunder had shouted that they ought to fight. But afterwards his old doubts had come sneaking up to assail him again, for Son-of-Thunder was afraid of war. He had never longed for places where the blood ran from people's open wounds.

But now around the fire he watched the warriors preparing themselves. He saw them painting their faces, tucking their loincloths into their belts to give more freedom for the dance. They put on the headbands they used in war, and braves with very long hair tied it up so that it should not get in the way. They donned their weapons as well and made ready to circle around the fire. Only in that way could they give a clear and definite answer. It was through the dance that they vowed to fight in the attack. He who danced was obliged to fight. He who held back would stay at home when the others went into battle.

Son-of-Thunder listened to the weird song of war and victory. His eyes were fixed on Pathfinder and he wondered how the medicine man had acquired all his knowledge of battle and blood.

No one could order the warriors to dance around the fire. Neither chief nor gods could command a N'de to fight. But Pathfinder could urge them, and Son-of-Thunder remembered how the medicine man had once lured Gray Warrior to approach the fire:

> *"Gray Warrior they call you.*
> *Gray Warrior they call you.*
> *They are calling on you,*
> *calling again and again.*
> *Will you fight or stay behind?*
> *Will you fight or stay behind?"*

And Gray Warrior, who would rather have stayed at home, had stood up unwillingly and joined the circle around the fire.

The dancers circled the flames four times. Then two danced off southward and two northward, and after that they changed places and repeated the steps three times more.

"Now the dance begins in earnest," thought Son-of-Thunder, "but I don't think Pathfinder will push me. I am not a warrior yet."

One of the women gave a long, drawn-out howl and other women followed her example. The howls echoed among the mountains, and the song grew louder.

Slowly the first warrior moved on to the meeting ground and circled the fire in time to the drums. Thus he gave his assent to go to war. One by one the braves followed his example, but Son-of-Thunder stood watching, hesitant. Some circled the fire only once; others danced around and around. They waved their weapons in the air, lunged and made threatening movements toward an invisible enemy. They practiced how they would fight at Arizpe. They slashed the air with sharp knives, bent their bows, took aim with the guns. The women kept up their howling and many of the spectators shouted to the dancers, urging them to attack, fight, and kill. The spectators shouted, but the dancers themselves were silent, for the N'de fight silently, and the dance represented the battle. The furious dance, said the N'de.

The song died down; the drumming slowed. Those who had danced went away from the fire and joined the spectators. They began to pray, and many lit cigarettes and pipes and blew out the smoke in the directions of the four winds. Son-of-Thunder felt the cool autumn night grow warm from the tobacco smoke.

The drumming increased in strength and tempo, and Pathfinder started to sing again. Other warriors circled the fire. One by one or in small groups they came from the circle of spectators. I want to fight too. We want to join the war dance. That was the meaning of the dance, of circling the flames.

Almost without noticing, Son-of-Thunder had tied his loincloth up in his belt and caught up his hair at the back with a small strap. He heard the drums, the song, the shouts and howls. He heard the mumble of prayers; the tobacco smoke stung his eyes. He remembered See-in-the-Dark singing, "It is better to have lightning in the hand than thunder in the mouth."

Then he entered the ring of warriors around the fire. In one hand he held his knife, in the other his fire-weapon. At first he moved quietly around the fire. But gradually his body fell into the rhythm of the song and the drums, first slowly, then faster and faster and later with violent, furious movements. He swung his fire-weapon, chopped at the air with his knife. He was dancer and he was warrior. War in dance, dance in war. Warrior and dancer, warrior and dancer!

✦ *The Long Line of Running Warriors*

They left at daybreak, all those who had circled the fire. They did not ride, they ran. Horses would merely be a hindrance now. Horses kicked up the dust and were easy to see in open terrain. Horses neigh and the sound of many hooves can be heard from afar. Horses have to be tended; they need food and rest. And they cannot climb rocks like goats, they cannot hide behind bushes like desert birds, they cannot dig themselves down into the sand like scorpions. But the N'de could do these things, and so they ran. Not in a big scattered flock, but in a long, long line, like a necklace drawn through the landscape.

The-One-Who-Yawns was leader, as the chiefs wished. It was he who had most to avenge. He had brought the message to the Chiricahua and Sierra Madre Mountains and afterwards he had traveled west to Arizpe alone. He had stayed for a week lying on a mountain ledge studying the area, watching the town and counting the Mexican soldiers when they rode in and out of the town gate.

Behind The-One-Who-Yawns ran Red Sleeves and all the Bedonkohe. Next came Juh and the Nedni, and in the rear Cochise and the Chokonen. Son-of-Thunder was almost the last in the line. His legs had found the rhythm, and his feet fell into the steps of the warrior in front of him, so that he trod in the same place as all the others. If anyone should cross the warriors' path it would be impossible for them to count how many had passed. Not even a N'de scout would guess correctly.

"There are five of them," he would say, "or perhaps ten or twenty."

But the braves numbered four hundred, and The-One-Who-Yawns led them westward and then southward. Son-of-Thunder breathed in the smell of sweat from the bodies in front of him. His eyes were lifted to the sky where the sun was almost hidden behind a cloud layer. There was a threat of storm in the air, a stifling clammy heat. And far to the southwest he saw the distant flashes of a thunderstorm brewing below the horizon.

They were in the Sierra Madre Mountains now and had been running for three days, eighty to a hundred kilometers from sunrise to sunset. They had slept when it grew dark, made short pauses during the day. They had eaten and drunk briefly. All carried light woollen blankets over their shoulders, and small bags of provisions. Their faces and bodies were painted. They were armed, and some also carried flints or fire-bits in their quivers, to make small fires for warming up their food. They had sat and eaten in silence. They made hardly a sound when they ran.

When the sun dipped in the west Son-of-Thunder could hear faint peals of thunder, and when they pitched camp in the evening he saw the streaks of the Thunder People's arrows. The-One-Who-Yawns knew rain was coming and he found a place under a big overhanging rock where the warriors could shelter. The chiefs stationed lookouts, and the thunder came nearer and nearer.

✦ The Face

Then the storm broke, with wind and pouring rain. Blue forked lightning struck at the ground with violent force and the thunderclaps echoed among the mountains.

The warriors huddled together beneath the overhang. They held their ears and prayed. They were afraid when the Thunder People came so close; they feared the death-dealing lightning. Many had rubbed themselves with sage juice. That should prevent madness, for thunder and lightning could send the N'de completely out of their minds.

But Son-of-Thunder stayed calm. Again he felt himself strangely drawn to the People up there in the clouds. He lay on his back with his hands at his sides and felt a kind of intoxication filling his whole body. Who were they, really, these giants of the sky? Where did they get their enormous powers?

He closed his eyes. The warriors prayed, and he heard the rumbling among the mountains from the deafening thunderclaps, heard the rain whipping the earth. Mother Earth must love thunderstorms; she must worship the life-giving water from the skies.

At first it was merely a dark mist which approached slowly, but then the fog shaped itself into an indistinct face with coarse features. It grew and grew, came nearer and nearer. But Son-of-Thunder was not afraid. He just waited. He wanted to see more. He concentrated on the features. Now he could also see the black hair and some of the heavy body. Now he could see the headband of lightning and the mouth of stardust. It opened, and the giant sang:

> *"I live in the clouds and I am sacred.*
> *I am Black Thunder.*
> *I make the earth fruitful.*
> *I send my lightning*
> *to give her life.*
> *I live in the clouds and I am sacred,*
> *Black Thunder, your father."*

The words sounded with the force of thunder, but the melody was tuneful. The giant repeated the song four times. Then the face faded again. It turned into mist and disappeared. But the words went on singing in Son-of-Thunder, over and over again. He wanted the giant to come back, for the face to show itself again. He lay for a long time with closed eyes, waiting, but nothing happened. When he opened them again the storm had abated. The last raindrops flew on the wind, and thunder and lightning passed on over the mountains.

Then Son-of-Thunder heard a groan of horror and pain. His body felt heavy and weak, but he stood up and in the darkness he made out a brave clutching his head while he rolled around on the ground. The man was Chokonen and Son-of-Thunder could hear Cochise shouting.

"The lightning shadow has got into Green Arrow! Can anyone help him?"

The others were standing up too, but they looked around and kept their distance from the maddened brave. Green Arrow bit at the wet earth, tore his hair, and rolled in the grass.

"Give me a cigarette," said Son-of-Thunder. "I will help him."

The braves stared in amazement at the young man who dared to answer, but one of them opened a leather bag and took out tobacco and an oak leaf. He rolled a cigarette and gave it to Son-of-Thunder. Another had found his flints and set light to some dry tinder beneath the overhang. Son-of-Thunder leaned down and lit the cigarette. Everyone looked at him. The dark figures stood unmoving, expectant.

Son-of-Thunder blew out the smoke in the directions of the four winds and named them by name, as he had heard the medicine men do during the ceremonies. Then he lifted his eyes to the skies and spoke.

"Before you did this to Green Arrow he was strong in body and mind. Now he is sick. I pray to you to blow a little of your spirit into this warrior so that he comes back to his senses."

The silent spectators could not see his eyes in the darkness, but many later said that that night Son-of-Thunder had been more god than man. Then he put one hand on the amulet hanging at his neck. With the other he drew out his knife and cut off a tiny piece of the amulet, a flake of it. He set fire to the flake with the cigarette and let it turn to ash in his hand. Then he bent down, dampened one of his fingertips on a wet blade of grass, and rubbed it into the ash.

"Hold him," he said.

Four braves threw themselves on Green Arrow. They held him on the ground with his face up. Son-of-Thunder sat down beside him and made the zigzag mark of lightning on his brow, over his cheek, down to the corner of his mouth.

Son-of-Thunder sang:

> *"He lives in the clouds and he is sacred.*
> *He is Black Thunder.*
> *He makes the earth fruitful.*
> *He sends his lightning*
> *and gives her life.*
> *He lives in the clouds and he is sacred,*
> *Black Thunder, my father."*

Four times did Son-of-Thunder sing, while his face turned toward all the corners of the universe. Then he rose to speak to the braves.

"You can let go of him now," he said.

The braves released their hold and stood up cautiously. For a while Green Arrow lay on the ground restlessly. Then he too got to his feet. He shook his head and shuffled off in a dazed way to the shelter of the overhang where he lay down quietly and fell asleep.

In the sky above, the last of the clouds disappeared and the moon shone down on the circle of braves standing in wonder around Son-of-Thunder. Cochise himself was among them and he smiled in astonishment into the night.

"My brother will never have any other name," he thought. "My brother will always be Son-of-Thunder."

✦ *Arizpe*

When Son-of-Thunder woke he smelled roasting meat. He sat up and rubbed the sleep out of his eyes. It was early morning and cold; the sun had not yet risen. Green Arrow sat a little way off, turning a spit over the heat of a small fire among the stones. Other braves were stirring as well.

Green Arrow greeted Son-of-Thunder.

"I have just shot a rabbit," he said. "Will you share the meat with me?"

"That will be good," said Son-of-Thunder.

He sat down on the other side of the fire. Green Arrow was in his forties. He had a name for being a skilled hunter and he had fought cunningly against the Mexicans for many years. He looked at Son-of-Thunder.

"Thank you for helping me," he said.

"It was the Thunder People who cured you," said Son-of-Thunder.

"I know, but they chose you to sing and pray."

"Yes, they chose me," said Son-of-Thunder thoughtfully.

Green Arrow had many amulets on leather thongs around his neck. Now he took one of them off. It was a piece of horn with small carvings on it, and he handed it to Son-of-Thunder.

"I would like you to have this," said Green Arrow. "The gods made me a hunter, and I have killed more creatures than others of my age. This amulet comes from the antler of the first stag I shot. It will bring you luck when you hunt. When we get back from Arizpe I will give you a good horse as well."

Son-of-Thunder thanked him for the gift and hung it around his neck. Then Green Arrow shared out the meat and they ate without further speech.

Some way off The-One-Who-Yawns sat with the three chiefs. They ate and talked in low voices, and Son-of-Thunder could see that The-One-Who-Yawns made signs on the ground with a sharp stick. The chiefs studied the signs carefully.

"It must be a map," thought Son-of-Thunder.

Soon after that the chiefs stood up, and The-One-Who-Yawns climbed up on to a big rock and spoke to the men.

"Warriors! Bedonkohe, Nedni, and Chokonen! Red Sleeves, Juh, and Cochise have asked me to lead you to Arizpe. I have kept watch on the town for seven days. I know the country, the hiding places and escape routes. I counted the soldiers. Now I have made a plan and the chiefs think we should do as I say. But if anything goes wrong, only those who raise their voices and say the plan is bad can reproach me afterwards."

The-One-Who-Yawns went over his plan in detail and the braves sat silently listening while he described how he thought the battle would go and how the Mexican soldiers would behave. When he was through, no one

stood up and said anything, for even though the plan
largely rested on one man's ability to read the thoughts
of the Mexican officers, and even if the battle should last
for three days, they felt they could rely now on this
Bedonkohe who had suffered so much that his face had
turned to stone.

The-One-Who-Yawns led them further south along the
western borders of the Sierra Madre Mountains. They
passed the Mexican town of Fronteras without being
seen. They began the descent toward the narrow valleys
of Sonora, ran in a wide circle around Nacozari and
crossed the river Yaqui. There were farms in the river
valley, and The-One-Who-Yawns sent scouts out ahead.
It was vital that the N'de were unobserved, vital that no
message was sent to the inhabitants of Arizpe warning
of the long line of warriors who were drawing nearer
and nearer . . .

That afternoon they reached the mountains on the
other side of the valley, and in the evening they had
passed the watershed and pitched camp under some
sparse trees on a hilltop.

Son-of-Thunder lay for a long time without sleeping.
He was not thinking of Arizpe and the coming battle.
He was not thinking of revenge, of the dead Bedonkohe, or of his first parents. Son-of-Thunder was thinking of the face in the mist, of the giant's song, and of
Green Arrow who had been freed from the perilous
lightning shadow.

"Giants in the skies," whispered Son-of-Thunder, "why
did you choose me?"

The next day they continued westward and began the descent to the long valley where the Sonora River winds along through a fertile landscape.

In the south the valley was wide and beautiful. The calm broad river flowed past the big town of Hermosillo and ran out into the Bay of California, whose vast waters only a few N'de had seen. The old people said that it stretched right to the places where life stops and the world runs into its last bend.

But further north the valley is narrower and in one place the river thunders along between sharp rocks and projections in a deep ravine. Before the river enters the ravine it meets another river. They are both broad, slow-flowing and shallow, and at this junction lies Arizpe.

Because the valley is fertile many people lived here. And behind the low city walls was quartered the largest garrison in this part of Mexico.

The ravine cut Arizpe off from speedy reinforcements from the south. To the north there were not many inhabitants and few peasants. To the west the land was flatter even though it bordered on mountains, and there were more farms. To the east a plain, a wood, and high wild cliffs lay close to the town. It was from this side that the braves of the three bands now approached.

There was no hurrying in Arizpe. Its people had plenty of time; life went on at a leisurely pace behind the walls. Bored soldiers sat outside the barracks, and the guards on the palisades gazed carelessly out over the Sonora Valley. Peasants worked in the fields and animals grazed peacefully. The tall grasses drank their last strength from the earth, still damp after the thunderstorm.

Arizpe had once been the capital of the Sonora province. The town had a wide plaza, and the yellow-brown buildings around it were stylish. Out in the square peasants and merchants sold their wares and little groups of men stood around talking. They wore big sombreros and ponchos of woven wool. Children played among the baskets and market stalls and the peasants swore at them when they grew too wild. By the water trough a mule was braying.

The commandant of the garrison, Colonel Galvez, strolled across the plaza. People greeted him respectfully as he passed and the colonel responded with a quick nod to left and right. He had a long, thin cigarillo in his mouth. Now and then he ran a finger along the dark curved scar on his right cheek. It was a bad habit he had acquired, but it had long been his custom. When peasants and soldiers mimicked him in the evenings, they always ran a finger slowly over their cheeks, almost affectionately.

Colonel Galvez was of middle height and his face had originally been quite ordinary and uninteresting. The scar had given him a kind of personality. It raised him out of the common mold and earned him respect from the soldiers, for they all knew he had won it in battle against the Apache. It was many, many years ago now. He had been an enlisted cavalryman under the command of Lieutenant Carasco, and the Apache had lured them into an ambush. Hand-to-hand fighting had followed and there had been heavy losses on both sides. Lieutenant Carasco lay on his back with a ferocious brave standing over him when Galvez had come to his rescue.

In the brief struggle that followed, the Apache's knife had bitten a deep gash in the young soldier's face. The wound had gone septic and the military doctor said it would never lose its dark color. From then on Galvez had loathed the Apache with all his heart.

But Lieutenant Carasco had given Galvez an outlet for his hatred. He had his rescuer promoted to sergeant, and together they had hunted down the "redskins" without mercy. Galvez could still remember how they had once led their men against a peaceful little camp in the place the Apache called the Rain Valley. A young mother had tried to flee with a tiny child in her arms. But all Apache were like snakes to Galvez. They were poisonous beasts that must be wiped out regardless of age and sex. He had shot the woman in the back and the brat had rolled off through the grass like a ball.

"Today it is nothing but a white skeleton," he thought.

Later on they had attacked another camp in the mountains north of Janos in Chihuahua province. There was really no point in this exercise, but Carasco had flown into a rage when he heard that the inhabitants of Janos were trading with the Apache. The soldiers had killed 130 Apaches and taken 90 prisoners they then sold as slaves to Mexican mining companies. The commandant in Janos had complained to the government, but the matter was hushed up. Now Carasco was a general and military governor of Sonora, while Galvez had risen through the ranks to become commandant of Arizpe.

The previous spring the inhabitants of Janos had made a new agreement with the Apache. Galvez had followed the example of his superior, crossed the border into Chihuahua province, and attacked the Apache camp.

Every person they caught was killed—the old, the women, and the children.

"Kill them!" Galvez had yelled to his soldiers. "Kill them!"

Now he walked across the plaza in his trim uniform and stroked his scar. He loved these morning walks through the town, loved the respect shown by the inhabitants.

"These people could not manage without me," he thought. "I am their great protector. The peasants could not cultivate the land and live their simple life without me. Here at Arizpe they feel safe. No Apache are brave enough to do battle against me and my soldiers."

He had crossed the plaza and was climbing the steps to the open door of his usual tavern when he heard the shouting. It came from the guard post on the eastern palisade.

"Apache!" came the cry. "Apache!"

✦ The Eight Soldiers

Everyone had heard the shouts. They each gazed anxiously at Colonel Galvez, who hurried back across the open square. The soldiers by the barracks stood up. They shouted to the guards.

"Are they attacking? Are there many of them?"

Galvez ran up the steps of the palisade. A guard saluted stiffly and briskly, passed him the telescope, and pointed east toward the wood on the other side of the plain. Galvez lifted the telescope and focused it.

There was no doubt. The small group of men over there were Apache. Galvez recognized them by their dress, by the long hair and the headbands. He tried to count them and made out ten. All were armed. He could not see any horses. The Apache just stood there, unmoving, with their faces turned toward Arizpe.

"What the hell are they standing there for?" muttered the colonel.

The N'de waited, and Son-of-Thunder was one of them. He had seen the figures up there behind the wall begin to move around, and he had heard the distant cries:

95

"Apache! Apache!" It was a word the enemy used, a Zuñi* word the N'de never uttered themselves.

Son-of-Thunder knew the plan; he was aware of what was about to happen. This time he did not stand at a safe distance guarding the horses. This time he was among the vanguard.

The ten warriors stood waiting, unmoving. The others were lying among the trees behind them. Before Son-of-Thunder had walked out of the wood Cochise had gripped his hands and looked deep into his eyes.

"Now you will be a warrior. Breathe calmly, think clearly," he had said.

Uncertainty began to spread in Arizpe. What did the warriors out there really want? Why were they just standing there? And were there really no more than ten, or were there others hiding in the woods and the mountains?

Colonel Galvez gave orders to strengthen the guards on the palisades all around the town. Then he summoned officers, noncommissioned officers, and the town's leading citizens to a meeting to discuss the situation. For a time the atmosphere was uneasy.

"Good Heavens!" exclaimed one of the townspeople. "We have four companies here, two of cavalry and two of infantry. There are ten savages out there. You cannot possibly think they represent a threat. Or can you, Colonel?"

Galvez stroked his scar. He thought of the massacre in the mountains north of Janos last year. Could this be the start of an act of revenge? "Hardly," he thought. An Apache band would never dare to mount an attack against

*Zuñi is the name of an Indian tribe of northern New Mexico..

Arizpe, for a band seldom had more than seventy or a hundred warriors. Besides, it was late in the autumn. An action for revenge would have come long ago, and Galvez had never heard of several bands joining up to fight together. The Apache were individualists; the bands roved around by themselves. They never knew of each other's movements.

Galvez thought a little longer. He had fought the Apache for many years, but there were still many bands he had never come across. These need not be Chihenne, Bedonkohe, Nedni, or Chokonen. They might be Apache from further west, north, or east, here to trade with the people of Arizpe, who did not dare to approach before they felt safe.

"Well, Colonel?" said the citizen impatiently.

"I think there are two possibilities," said Galvez. "The first is that the Apache want to talk to us or trade with us."

"And the second?"

"The second possibility is that the warriors out there want to distract our attention."

"From what?"

"From the farms west or south of the town. Those men out there are merely part of a larger band who intend to steal horses, mules, and cattle from the peasants. They expect us to send soldiers out to investigate, and when the soldiers get near them they will fire off a few shots before they run off, hoping we will take up the chase. And while they lead us off through the woods and up into the mountains, their main force will plunder the farms."

The men nodded. They had faith in Galvez and they thought what he had just said sounded sensible.

"What will we do, Colonel?" one of them asked.

Galvez turned to a junior officer.

"You, Second Lieutenant, take forty men out by the west gate and warn the peasants. Bring the women and children into the town and post men on the farms."

"And you, Sergeant," he continued, addressing a non-commissioned officer, "take seven men and ride out toward the ten warriors through the east gate. Take a white flag with you. That will show them you are on a peaceful mission. Find out what they want. If they turn and run, you will know the whole thing is a distracting maneuver. Do not follow them but hurry to the farms."

It was late in the day, and Son-of-Thunder gazed at the sky. In the autumn air migrating geese were etched against it clearly. The birds winged southward like a great V, and he could hear their excited honking. The grass on the plain was still tall, but in the woods the trees wore their autumn colors.

Suddenly one of the warriors called out quietly, "Look, here they come!"

The heavy wooden gates in the town wall slowly opened and for a while the warriors could see the houses nearest to them. Then the soldiers came in sight. There were eight of them in all and they rode in pairs. One of them held a long pole with a white cloth high in the air, just as The-One-Who-Yawns had said. The doors closed behind them and they rode out into the shallow river. The horses neighed and hooves splashed the water. Son-of-Thunder still stood unmoving among the braves, but his heart beat faster and his muscles were tensed. He drew deep breaths as Cochise had told him. He tried to control his nervousness, conquer his fear.

"Keep calm, keep calm," he thought.

The soldiers reached the other bank of the river and rode up on to the plain. The sunlight flashed on bridles and spurs. They came nearer and nearer.

Sergeant Medina tried to smile. He urged his horse slowly forward. Then he threw a glance up at the white flag beside him, as if to reassure himself. He stared at the Apache. He could not yet see their faces clearly.

"Smile, lads," he growled, "smile, for God's sake."

He tried to make out a leader, a chief, among them. His gaze moved from one to the next of the ten braves, but he could not see any one different from the rest. There were less than twenty meters to go and now he could see their faces. They were solemn. Suddenly the sergeant felt that something was not right, did not make sense. Fifteen meters more. He raised his right hand, waved and signaled. Why did none of them move forward? Ten meters. He prepared to stop his horse.

From the woods behind them came the signal they had been waiting for, the hawk's cry of The-One-Who-Yawns, and Son-of-Thunder promptly threw himself flat on the ground. He knew the others did likewise. Then the crash of hundreds of rifle shots came through the trees. Bullets and arrows found their marks and the air was filled with death. The whole thing was over in seconds.

Then Son-of-Thunder leaped to his feet and rushed at the soldiers with lifted knife. But they all lay in the grass, and they were all dead. The white flag was dyed red with blood.

✦ All Eyes Filled with Fear

The soldiers and officers in Arizpe stood as if thunderstruck on the east palisade. It had all happened so fast; it had been so horrific. Some crossed themselves, while others swore quietly and helplessly.

Colonel Galvez had turned pale and his forefinger rubbed frantically at the scar. Then a whole army of Apache warriors came out of the shadows among the trees. He saw them robbing the dead soldiers of arms and ammunition.

"Will they scalp them?" asked the man next to the colonel.

"Apache don't take scalps," replied Galvez irritably.

Then the braves vanished into the woods again and shortly afterwards they were swarming like ants up through the stones and rocks of the mountainside.

"Count them!" roared Colonel Galvez. "Count them!"

Officers and soldiers aimed their telescopes at the mountain and tried to count. Galvez was shaking. It had been a shock to see the eight soldiers suddenly mown down out there. But it was also the trick they had played on him, anger and humiliation that made the colonel tremble.

"There are several hundred of them," said one of the soldiers.

"Get it exactly! Count properly!"

"Three hundred and fifty, Sir. More perhaps."

"Between three and five hundred, Sir. It's hard to say. They move so fast."

Most of the Apache vanished into a cleft far up on the mountainside, but some stayed to keep guard. One of the warriors pointed out lookout places on mountain ledges and big rocks for the others to station themselves on. Galvez could see him through his telescope. It was a long way away and the colonel's hands were still shaking. But he could make out the warrior's features. His mouth was a long, thin lipless line.

The braves came to a halt on a heather-clad plateau among sharp peaks. There was no laughing. They did not celebrate victory, for this was merely the beginning. They rested and some of them had something to eat. Others saw to their weapons, and the sun sank in the western sky.

The-One-Who-Yawns had stayed out on the mountainside with the lookouts. He had waited a long time, reassuring himself that the soldiers in Arizpe did not take up the pursuit. Now he came calmly running up to the warriors on the plateau. The sky was red, and once again he climbed onto a rock and spoke to them. His words shone like torches in the autumn evening. He praised the ten who had stood unwavering and waited; he praised the marksmen among the trees. He talked of the Mexican soldiers and his voice shook with scorn.

"They killed more than a hundred defenseless Bed-onkohe in the mountains north of Janos," he said.

"They mutilated our women and our children. And today, what did they do today? They showed us a white cloth tied to a pole. Do they not know we are men? Do they not know we are N'de? Do they not know our hearts are calling out for revenge? Can a white cloth fastened to a pole stop a Chokonen, a Nedni, a Bedonkohe?"

"No!" shouted the warriors. "No! No! No!"

Chief Red Sleeves stood up. His body was like a mountain, his voice like an avalanche of stones. He pointed at The-One-Who-Yawns.

"Braves!" he began. "This Bedonkohe has praised us, and it is right that we did as we should do. But it was his plan we followed; without his advice the eight Mexi-can soldiers would not now lie dead. We have taken some revenge, but tomorrow the warfare must go on, tomorrow more soldiers will die. Should we follow this man's plan?"

"Yes!" yelled the braves. "Yes! Yes! Yes!"

That night Son-of-Thunder thought about the dead soldiers in the grass. How simple it was to kill, then, how simple it was to silence human hearts. He saw the twisted uniform-clad bodies, the wide-open eyes, the great bleed-ing wounds where the bullets had struck. Yes, the N'de had won victory today, but tomorrow he would again be among the foremost in the field. Son-of-Thunder felt no happiness, for he was sick at heart. He thought of his first parents, of Swift Deer and Little Eagle, whom he had seen in a dream after Nachi died.

"Are you not avenged now?" he thought.

Then he fell asleep.

But in Arizpe hardly anyone slept. The women gathered in the church to kneel and pray. Soldiers lay sleepless in their bunks in the barracks, and all eyes were filled with fear. Panic lurked. What would happen next?

Colonel Galvez and his men sat around a table in the officers' mess. They tried to make plans for the next day—an almost impossible task. All they knew was that the Apache had lookouts on the mountainside. That meant they did not intend to leave and that they would attack again. And there were many hundreds of them. Would they dare an attack on the town?

"I hate them," thought Colonel Galvez. "Oh, how I hate them!"

✦ An Attack on the Town from the South or the West?

Son-of-Thunder was woken by Cochise before dawn. There was moonlight and no wind.

"You must wake up," whispered Cochise. "The-One-Who-Yawns is waiting for us. We are off soon."

Son-of-Thunder got up and rolled up his blanket. Around him on the plateau most of the braves were still asleep. The few who were to go had gathered around a small fire. Cochise and Son-of-Thunder went up to them and sat down.

"Good, we are all here now," said The-One-Who-Yawns. His face was red in the firelight. "You know what is going to happen. All the same I will run through the plan once more."

Nineteen warriors sat around the flames listening. When The-One-Who-Yawns had finished, they rose and followed him at a run, down from the plateau, through the darkness. They reached the cleft from where they could see the lights of Arizpe. Son-of-Thunder knew that on the west palisade the Mexican soldiers were straining their eyes into the night and listening. The-One-Who-Yawns hooted softly like an owl; answering calls came from the lookouts.

Cautiously he led the braves down among the stones of the mountain slope. They reached the wood and ran on along the wide path the Mexicans had once cut between the trees. When they had almost reached the plain The-One-Who-Yawns stopped.

"This is the place," he whispered. "Hide yourselves, wait for the signal, and keep as still as stones."

The warriors vanished like shadows into the night. They dispersed themselves and hid among the trees on the north side of the path. Cochise and Son-of-Thunder slid in among the trees on the south side.

"Good luck, Brother," said the chief.

Then he vanished too.

Son-of-Thunder took a few steps, crouched down behind a bush, and made himself one with the dark leaves.

Then began a long wait, and while he waited Son-of-Thunder listened to the night voices of nature, to the distant howl of coyote, to the rustling nearby of a field mouse through the grass.

Daylight slowly filled the eastern sky and the officers on the palisade peered toward the wood and the mountainside. Their faces bore the marks of a sleepless night.

Colonel Galvez strained his eyes through his telescope. He could see nothing among the trees, but suddenly he caught sight of an Apache warrior half-hidden behind a rock on the mountainside. He slowly moved the telescope and picked out another, then one more, then many.

"Can you see them, Sir?"

"Yes, I see them. Count them."

The officer counted.

"About 150, Sir."

"Same here, Sir."

Galvez lowered his telescope and looked around his officers.

"Well?" he said. "And what does that mean?"

"It means several hundred are missing, Sir."

"So?" said Galvez.

The senior officer of the two infantry companies, Lieutenant Malgares, shrugged his shoulders.

"A new distracting maneuver," he said. "No doubt about it in my opinion, Sir."

Galvez nodded. He had had the same idea himself but wanted someone else to give voice to it. He had been so definite in his views the previous day, and he had been wrong. Now he feared to make a new blunder.

"And where is their main force now?" he asked.

"They will hardly be in the woods," replied the lieutenant.

Again Galvez agreed, but he wanted the trust of the other officers when he came to a decision.

"Why not?" he said.

"The Apache clearly want to get us to go out of town," said Lieutenant Malgares, "but they do not dare to fight down here in the lowlands. They always choose a surprise attack. Down here a battle could easily lead to a war of attrition, and the Apache know we have enough ammunition for several weeks. True, many of them have guns, but their big problem is still the lack of shot and powder."

"Excellent, Lieutenant," exclaimed Galvez. "You took the words straight out of my mouth. So then, the main force?"

"As you know, there is a descent from the mountains further south," said Malgares. "I think most of the Apache will be there now, Sir. I think they are planning an attack on the town from south or west, perhaps both. Their plan is to strike while we are occupied with fighting the 150 warriors up there on the mountainside."

A sergeant asked to speak.

"If the Apache are planning an attack on the town from south or west, we can just stay here with our whole force and wait for them," he said optimistically.

Galvez looked at him scornfully.

"Do you agree with the sergeant, Lieutenant?"

"By no means," said the lieutenant. "If we stay in here behind the walls the Apache will merely wait."

"In other words, we will then be besieged," said Galvez, and now he had regained his self-confidence. He stroked the scar. "While the Apache are waiting for us to run out of supplies they themselves can hunt and get the food they need. Those savages out there are snakes, and we know snakes are patient. In 1837 the Apache laid siege to Santa Rita del Cobre for a whole month and we all know how that tale ended. Do you want to be besieged, Sergeant?"

The sergeant shook his head shamefacedly and reddened.

Galvez looked at Lieutenant Malgares again.

"Then," said the colonel, "may I make the following suggestion: you, Lieutenant, will lead the infantry across the plain and into the wood. Take two of the howitzers with you. When the Apache are within range, you open fire immediately. Take plenty of ammunition with you. Agreed?"

"Fully agreed," smiled Malgares. "I assume that you yourself intend to post cavalrymen on the palisades?"

"You can be sure of that," said Galvez. "The Apache do not know much about this garrison. When they see you leave they will think the town is practically emptied of soldiers. When the attack comes we'll give them a welcome they never dreamed of."

✦ The Mules

But Colonel Galvez was mistaken. Less than a month before, The-One-Who-Yawns had lain on the mountain ledge for a week. He had watched the town and counted the soldiers. Then he had made a plan; he had read the commandant's thoughts long before he had thought them.

The gates were opened, Lieutenant Malgares gave the command to advance, and the two lines of foot soldiers moved off. In the middle of the column four horses drew a large wagon. The two howitzers had been placed on it under a tarpaulin. A soldier brought up the rear leading four mules loaded with ammunition.

The lieutenant was the only mounted man. He drove his horse toward the river, and while the hooves splashed out into the cool water he gave a new command. The soldiers held their guns above their heads with both hands and followed him. Two by two they waded across in water up to their waists.

Colonel Galvez watched the advance from the palisades. It was midday; scattered fleecy clouds hardly moved across the sky. The two companies of infantry reached the other side of the river and Lieutenant Malgares led them eastward through the tall grass of the plain. Galvez thought it a beautiful sight.

Son-of-Thunder lay behind the bush. The only thing about him that moved was his eyes. A double dove's coo rolled softly through the trees. It was The-One-Who-Yawns signaling that the soldiers were on their way, and Son-of-Thunder sent up a silent prayer, not for his own life, but for victory. He prayed to Usen that the plan would succeed.

Twigs crackled, birds flew off, and the soldiers came into sight on the path. Only one was mounted. The others were on foot, but they did not walk in the way Mexicans usually did. They tramped along, their boots thundered upon the ground, and Son-of-Thunder knew this was what they called marching.

The soldiers passed through the wood only twenty paces away, and Son-of-Thunder counted them. They numbered two hundred. All carried fire-weapons in their hands and blue-knives* in their belts. Four horses pulled a large wagon and he pondered on what was concealed under the tarpaulin. Although the soldiers were marching they kept a watchful lookout around them, and Son-of-Thunder hardly dared breathe.

Suddenly he smiled. For behind the two ranks, led on a long rope by a single soldier, came four mules laden with heavy boxes exactly as The-One-Who-Yawns

*blue-knife = bayonet.

had described. The mules made heavy weather of the load and were lagging behind the soldiers. Cautiously Son-of-Thunder changed position and made ready.

The One-Who-Yawns was one with a tree. He caught the smell of mules, saw the soldier trying to make them speed up.

The Bedonkohe's right hand closed around the shaft of his flint knife. Slowly he pulled it out of its sheath under his belt. At the same time he filled his lungs with air and pursed his mouth. For the second time the double dove's coo sounded from the narrow lips.

Then he rushed out with knife raised, and leaped like a stag through the grass toward the soldier.

Son-of-Thunder jumped up when he heard the signal. His feet carried him at furious speed toward the mules. Cochise was beside him. They saw The-One-Who-Yawns throw himself at the soldier and the knife pierce deep into the soldier's body.

Son-of-Thunder reached the animals. He bent quickly, tore the rope from the hand of the dead soldier, turned the first mule, and hauled it after him. Cochise urged on the other with a branch. They kicked out with their back legs. The-One-Who-Yawns vanished among the trees. All happened fast.

Then they heard the enemy cry, "Apache! Apache!"

They were discovered, and Son-of-Thunder saw that the last soldiers in the column had turned around. They fell to their knees and raised their fire-weapons. For a moment he felt the world stand still. Then the shots thundered from the hidden warriors' fire-weapons, from tree-tops and bushes on the north side of the path. The soldiers flung out their arms and fell.

"Run!" yelled Cochise.

Son-of-Thunder dragged at the rope and the mules followed him, throwing themselves from side to side and kicking up into the air. The wood was full of shots and shrieks.

"Faster!" yelled Cochise and beat the mules hard on their flanks.

The warriors up on the mountainside had begun to shoot as well. Now the soldiers came under double fire, and Son-of-Thunder ran and ran, south between the trees and out on to the plain, away from the bullets.

Colonel Galvez clenched his hands on the parapet of the city wall. His nails scraped the hard yellow-brown clay; the knuckles were white. He snarled with rage and despair.

Far out on the plain, south of the woods, the four mules trotted off between two Apache warriors. They made their way toward the other pass into the mountains.

"The ammunition," groaned Galvez. "The ammunition."

"Should we send the cavalry after them, Sir?" shouted a guard.

"It is too late," whispered the colonel in a tear-choked voice. "Can't you see it is too late, damn you?"

✦ The-One-Who-Yawns Gets a New Name

Lieutenant Malgares had jumped down from his horse. The bullets whistled around him and he took shelter between two thick oak trunks. He roared to the soldiers, "Company One! Fire at the men on the mountainside! Prepare the howitzers! Company Two! Fire at the snipers in the wood!"

The responses came through the reports of the guns.

"Very good, Lieutenant!"

"Very good, Lieutenant!"

A fearful thought struck Malgares. Suppose the main force of the Apache were behind the trees and bushes in the woods?

"How many of them are in there?" he shouted.

"We don't know, Lieutenant! The firing has stopped!"

Malgares ventured out from his hiding place. Firing continued, but the shots came from Company One and from the mountainside. The soldiers of Company Two were waiting. They were on bended knee or lying down, peering intently in among the tree trunks.

"Should we go after them, Lieutenant? Should we move back through the wood?" shouted a sergeant.

Malgares tried to think. Why had the braves stopped firing?

Suddenly one of the soldiers pointed and shouted, "There's one!"

The lieutenant caught a brief glimpse of a lithe warrior leaping bent over from one tree to another. Shots roared but missed him.

"He is behind the tree over there!" shouted the sergeant.

"Fire when he comes out again!"

The soldiers waited, their guns at the ready. Behind them firing continued between Company One and the warriors on the mountain. Some were trying to get the howitzers off the wagon. The horses whinnied and dragged at the shafts. The back leg of one of them had been shot.

Lieutenant Malgares had seen the running warrior's face. It was hard and it reminded him of a picture he had been afraid of as a child. The picture had hung on the wall of a room in his parents' house, and it represented The Holy Hieronymus.

"Hey, Geronimo!" shouted Malgares. "Come out of there!"

And suddenly there he was again, the same warrior, but by a different tree. The soldiers aimed again and fired. Once more they missed, and once again the warrior vanished. The men in uniform swore.

"How the hell did he do it?"

But now they had tasted blood.

"Geronimo!" they yelled. "Show yourself, Geronimo!"

The-One-Who-Yawns froze for a moment behind the tree trunk, then sank down flat in the grass and crawled backwards. He came to a thicket and stood up behind another tree. He could not see them, but he knew the other braves were very close.

"Away with you now!" he whispered.

He heard how the grass rustled quietly and knew they had gone. Just as Son-of-Thunder and Cochise had vanished with the mules.

He waited until the braves had a reasonable head start, then showed himself to the soldiers again. They fired and fired, but The-One-Who-Yawns was lithe and swift as a mountain lion.

"Now I will disappear too," he thought.

And soon he was running south over the plain. Far away in front of him he saw the backs of the running warriors, and when he reached the pass into the mountains they stood smiling and waiting for him. Cochise and Son-of-Thunder were there too. They raised their weapons and swung them above their heads.

"Geronimo!" they shouted. "Geronimo! Geronimo! Geronimo!"

The-One-Who-Yawns was no more.

✦ Don't Speak of the Dead

The snipers had killed eight of Lieutenant Malgares's soldiers and later twenty had fallen to bullets and arrows from the mountainside. An equal number were seriously or slightly wounded.

Company Two had thoroughly searched the wood, but both Geronimo and the others seemed to have sunk into the ground. So then Malgares had directed all his forces into the struggle against the braves on the mountainside. The sound of gunfire filled the air, the howitzers thundered, and gunpowder smoke lay thick among the trees. The cannons were aimed high and the cannonballs often loosened landslides where they struck. Big rocks threatened to crush the Apache, but they went on fighting.

"I think the savages have been sent reinforcements, Sir!" shouted one of the noncommissioned officers. "They are all over the place up there!"

And only then did Malgares realize that he was no longer fighting against 150 warriors, but the whole great Apache force. He crouched on his knees, half-hidden behind a fallen tree trunk, some way behind the fighting soldiers.

"Are we keeping them at a distance?" he shouted.

"They keep coming closer, Sir! And we haven't a lot more ammunition!"

Malgares swore quietly and gave thought to the problem. He saw two possibilities. He could send a party to Arizpe to ask for reinforcements and ammunition. On the other hand he had need of every single man. The other possibility was to withdraw with all his forces. He had about 150 unharmed fighting men left, while the Apache might have 500. The day was far spent and up there in the mountains the mules were no doubt tethered by now. The Apache had shot and powder for many days' fighting.

"They are still closer now, Sir!"

Then Malgares made a decision.

"Get the howitzers up on the wagon!" he ordered. "Return fire and slowly retreat!"

That night the N'de buried their seven dead among the stones and lit great fires in the wood. Close relatives of the dead cut their hair short, and those who had brought in the bodies washed themselves in a stream. But no mourning songs were heard among the trees, for Chokonen, Nedni, and Bedonkohe never sang for the dead.

Cochise and Son-of-Thunder sat by themselves. They had wrapped their blankets around them and sat with their backs against an oak. The crickets sang; the fireflies shone in the darkness. Son-of-Thunder thought of the lifeless bodies under the stones and he knew they were not feeling the cold.

"You are a warrior now, Son-of-Thunder," said Cochise quietly. "The fighting will continue tomorrow, but you have already proved yourself. Today you carried out a deed that will be remembered."

"Why did Geronimo choose me?" asked Son-of-Thunder. "Was it you who told him I could run?"

"Yes, I told him. I know of no swifter runner than you."

"My first father was swifter," said Son-of-Thunder thoughtfully.

Cochise said nothing. A chill westerly wind rustled the leaves above them.

"Don't let us speak of the dead," he said.

Then Son-of-Thunder turned to his brother and looked him straight in the eyes.

"My first father is not dead," he said. "My first father runs over the prairies in the green country beneath the earth."

✦ The Man with the Scar

At nine o'clock the next morning Colonel Galvez made the most important decision of his life.

Up to now the Apache had had the upper hand. First they had killed the eight soldiers. Then they had stolen the ammunition and caused heavy losses among the infantry companies, all because Galvez had allowed himself to be tricked by the Apache's wily plan. But now it was the colonel's turn to embark on tactics and strategy. Now he would decide how the battle was to be fought.

"This time we will fight in my way," he thought.

Then he gave orders to prepare for battle and at nine-thirty precisely he inspected the four companies. The infantrymen stood rigidly to attention with newly polished boots and well-greased guns. This time there were four howitzers, and new horses waited in front of the wagons. The cavalrymen, the colonel's pride and joy, sat straight-backed in their saddles. Their guns were in the saddle holsters and long polished swords hung from their belts. The cool westerly breeze played in the horses' manes and tails. Every one of Arizpe's fighting fit officers and men were ranked on the parade ground, and Galvez made a speech.

He did not mention his defeats of the last two days, and barely mentioned the dead men. Colonel Galvez talked of Mexico, their fatherland, and the beautiful Sonora province. He talked of the peasants' efforts to make a fruitful garden out of the land and of the necessary presence of the military for this to be achieved. He said that the greatest impediment to the Sonora region becoming the pride of the nation was the presence of the barbaric savages, who roamed the mountains half-naked and lived like animals. He spoke of their heathen customs, their superstitions and unlimited wickedness, of the necessity of driving them out and killing them.

"Today," he concluded, "we will show these fiends that we are masters in this land. Our entire force is going out on to the plain. We will attack the wood, meet them face to face and at the end of the day we will be victorious. It they take refuge in the mountains, but then return, we will drive them off once more. For no Apache can fight in open country. They are too cowardly for that."

Then Colonel Galvez put his boot into the stirrup and mounted his great white stallion. He raised his sword.

"Soldiers!" he shouted. "For Mexico and Sonora!"

"For Mexico and Sonora!" came the cry in unison from four hundred soldiers.

And so at precisely ten o'clock the gates were opened and the long columns left the town and crossed the river. The infantry marched first, led by Lieutenant Malgares on horseback. Then came the wagons with howitzers and eight mules carrying ammunition. Next rode Colonel Galvez and the two long lines of cavalrymen.

When they had reached the plain the officers gathered together and studied the wood through their telescopes. Among the trees they could see the Apache waiting with guns and bows at the ready.

"Forward at the double!" ordered Lieutenant Malgares.

"Forward at jog trot!" roared Colonel Galvez.

But not all the N'de were waiting in the wood. Most of them lay side by side in the tall grass that waved like a sea in the western wind. Geronimo had read the commandant's thoughts, and the warriors had lain in wait since before dawn. Together they formed a great horseshoe stretching from the wood far out on the plain. The unsuspecting soldiers stormed straight into this horseshoe.

Son-of-Thunder pressed his body flat against the ground. He felt the grass blades against his face. He heard the soldiers' boots and the horses' hooves thundering upon the earth. He heard the big heavy animals snorting while their riders urged them on across the plain toward the wood. He held his weapon in front of him in the grass; at his side were bow and lance. His war club hung at his belt, and his knife was free in its sheath.

"I will fight like a mountain lion," he said to himself, "as I fought the old oak tree at home in the Chiricahua Mountains."

Then the warriors in the wood began to shoot. Son-of-Thunder leaped to his feet. This was the signal he had waited for. He placed the butt of his gun against his shoulder, sighted, and pulled the trigger. The cavalryman was hurled out of his saddle and flung to the ground. Son-of-Thunder threw down his fire-weapon and put an arrow to his bow.

The attack came as a complete surprise to the Mexicans. A wall of warriors rose up on both sides of the column. Hundreds of Apache guns thundered; soldiers and horses crashed to the ground. A rain of arrows followed the bullets and more fell.

"Retreat! Retreat!" roared Colonel Galvez with panic in his voice.

But no one heard him in the melee and retreat was impossible. The horseshoe changed into an oval, with the warriors closed in around the enemy.

"We are surrounded, Sir!"

"We are surrounded!"

"Shoot!" yelled Galvez. "Fire!"

Total confusion followed. From all sides at once Apache came rushing with lances, knives, and clubs. The terrified soldiers were confronted with war-painted faces, glances of fiery lightning.

Man struggled against man, but the Mexicans had lost almost half their number. The surviving infantrymen tried to fix their bayonets but failed. They used their rifle butts instead. And the cavalrymen tried to slash with their swords. Some of them were still on their horses, but the Apache rushed up and dragged them to the ground. The Mexicans fought for their lives.

Son-of-Thunder fought for his life as well. He, who had longed for a valley with cool springs and peaceful plains, was in the midst of the battle. His club struck a soldier on a rearing horse, his lance plunged into another. He raised his knife, met an assault, chopped, and ran. Sweat poured from him and his skin shone.

And then suddenly he was standing face to face with a Mexican chief. A tall, powerful man with stars on his uniform tunic and a dark curved scar on one cheek. The officer stood still, his long knife held out like a lance in front of him. It dripped blood. A few meters away a white stallion lay struggling with death.

Their eyes met. They sized each other up. The older, experienced soldier against the lithe, inexperienced warrior.

At first they stood still, but slowly Son-of-Thunder began to circle around the man with the scar. He bent his body and moved sideways, feeling his way forward with his feet. His short knife was raised to strike. The officer stood still, following Son-of-Thunder's movements. All the time they looked straight into each other's eyes.

Son-of-Thunder concentrated on this alone, on what he had learned: to wait for a lunge, to leap to one side, to avoid the opponent's weapon, to turn swiftly, to strike with the knife.

And so, in the brief moment before the jab came, Son-of-Thunder saw the infinitesimal twitch on the officer's face. He threw himself to one side, leaned his whole body weight on his right foot, whirled around, and sent his knife curving like lightning at the enemy's back.

Colonel Galvez was dead.

The surviving soldiers had taken refuge on a small rise on the north of the plain. There were not many of them but they loaded and fired, loaded and fired, and one Nedni was hit in the chest.

Then Son-of-Thunder heard Geronimo's voice.

"Fall off, warriors! We have avenged! Let us not lose more of our own!"

So they ran through the grass toward the wood and the mountains.

Five days later they neared the camp and sent up smoke signals to show they were coming. Up in the mountains the women, children, and old people began to adorn themselves to greet the warriors who would soon be back with them. When they arrived, there was weeping for those who had fallen and rejoicing at the great victory over the Mexicans.

✦ The Giant

The first night after the Chokonen returned to the Chiricahua Mountains, the giant showed himself to Son-of-Thunder in a dream. This time his face was clearly visible, and Son-of-Thunder could see not only his head-band of lightning and his mouth of stardust, but also his wise eyes of a thousand raindrops. They were like ponds at sunrise.

The giant's eyes did not look at Son-of-Thunder. They gazed past him, and in the dream the young warrior turned and caught sight of three people on a plain. First he saw the dead officer with the dark curved scar. He lay on his side with an open wound between his shoulder blades, and the grass around him was dry and withered.

But further off, where the grass blades were green and full of sap and the flowers bloomed in splendid colors, a man and woman of the N'de clan ran slowly over the plain, as if hovering. They were Swift Deer, Son-of-Thunder's first father, and Little Eagle, Son-of-Thunder's first mother.

About the Author

Stig Holmås is a Norwegian librarian who has "spent a lifetime" studying the Chiricahua bands of the Apache and visiting all the sites he describes in this book. *Son-of-Thunder* was named the "Best Book for Children and Young People" by the Norwegian Ministry of Culture and has been translated into English, Swedish, Danish, and German.

Other Fine Quality Childrens' Books from Harbinger House

WALKER OF TIME
by Helen Hughes Vick

A compelling, fact-based mystery about a teenage Hopi Indian boy who "time travels" back to the final days of his ancestors in the cliff-dwellings of northern Arizona, in A.D. 1250.

Ages 12 and up
ISBN 0-943173-80-9 $9.95 paperback
ISBN 0-943173-84-1 $15.95 hardcover

A KIDS' GUIDE TO BUILDING FORTS
by Tom Birdseye
illustrated by Bill Klein

From a blanket over the dining room table to dome forts, igloos, lean-tos, and a dozen more in all climates and environments, this hand-lettered, illustrated guide shows kids how to create their own secret place.

Ages 8–14
ISBN 0-943173-69-8 $8.95 paperback

OUTDOOR SURVIVAL HANDBOOK FOR KIDS
by Willy Whitefeather

From treating a bee sting to building an overnight shelter, this practical, easy-to-follow handbook gives children the knowledge and confidence they need to survive outdoors.

All Ages
ISBN 0-943173-47-7 $8.95 paperback